D0966026

VOYAGE
to the BOTTOM
of the SEA

Authorized Edition

by RAYMOND F. JONES

illustrations by
LEON JASON STUDIOS

WHITMAN PUBLISHING COMPANY • Racine, Wisconsin

Dedicated to

Mary Lynne

Copyright © 1965 by
Cambridge Productions, Inc.
and Twentieth Century-Fox Television, Inc.
All rights reserved throughout the world.
Printed in U.S.A. by Western Printing
and Lithographing Company

CONTENTS

1

Sea Baby

THE SEA mothered the giant gray submarine. With easy strength it lifted the vessel on long, rolling waves, then plunged it beneath the surface, only to raise it once more and bathe it in whitecaps and spray.

Captain Lee Crane stood at the huge, square observation ports in the bow of the *Seaview* and watched the breaking waves expectantly. At each plunge the water surged over the ports and drowned the world outside. Then, as the ship lifted, the water drained in shining cascades and sunlight poured in.

As Captain Crane watched, he kept an ear cocked to the intercom speaker above his head. Suddenly the crashing water did not drain away and leave the ports shining and transparent. A brownish darkness clung, and sunlight came through with amber dullness.

Crane grasped the microphone and signaled the turbine room. "Quarter speed!" To the helmsman, he ordered, "Full rudder, right!"

The *Seaview* turned slowly as each smashing wave darkened the ports more. From the other side of the observation room Admiral Harriman Nelson nodded approval of the maneuver.

"We'll have to dry-dock for a month to clean the hull if that stuff builds up," Nelson said.

"We're still miles from Oil City Eighteen," said Crane. "The oil slick has spread farther than we thought. But obviously it's only on the surface. The column of oil coming up from the seabed must be quite narrow. I'm going down in order to approach without running through this stuff."

"I think you're right," said Nelson. "But first I'd like to take a look around from periscope height, if you don't mind."

"Certainly."

Captain Crane switched on the electronic periscope that transferred an image from its eye high above the sea to the screen of the observation room. From the remote-control panel Crane rotated the periscope eye slowly. As far as they could see in the direction of their former course the water was black and dead, with a heavy pool of oil that lay many feet deep on the surface. The oil was swiftly spreading its black cloud over the clean water of the sea.

Here and there clusters of floating debris dotted the oily surface. Pieces of submarine houses, furniture, machinery. And bodies. The two men knew that scores of human bodies of oilmen and their families were out there. It was doubtful that anyone had survived the disaster of Oil City Eighteen. Crane turned off the periscope.

"There were six oil wells down there," said Nelson. "They each flowed at an average of a hundred and ten barrels of crude oil per hour. If they're all ruptured there's going to be oil over half the South Atlantic before they're recapped."

"It'll hit the central African beaches in a day

or two," said Crane. "I wonder if it shouldn't be ignited to get rid of it."

"Not until we know what villages may be in the path of the current. They'd have to be evacuated. Let's see what's down below first."

They knew what was down below, Crane thought. Disaster. Death.

Two days ago there had been a thriving oil city on the continental shelf nine hundred feet below the surface, a hundred and twenty miles off the central African coast. Then a submarine earthquake had ripped the seabed. Within moments Oil City Eighteen had ceased to exist. Only a single frantic cry from the radio operator had given the outside world any warning.

There was no sign of survivors. Only the gusher of black, thick oil that spewed up from the depths gave evidence that man had ever touched the seabed there. The radio operator's cry had set in motion orders from Washington to the Nelson Institute of Marine Research, proprietors of the great research submarine *Seaview*. Fortunately the ship had been cruising off the coast of Spain when the message came through. It was requested to put in at Gibraltar to pick up a geological expert who was being flown from New York, then proceed to the disaster site and investigate, and evacuate any survivors.

Much of the thick oil had washed from the *Seaview's* ports as the ship wheeled around. But now, as the submarine descended into the depths, daylight dimmed and the ports darkened.

Crane switched on the powerful searchlights in the bow of the ship. Schools of brightly colored fish darted in terror from the sudden intrusion.

From the rear of the observation room a figure arose and walked slowly forward. Dr. Robert Banks, the expert in submarine geology, had been aboard many submarines. He had descended to the depths in bathyspheres and diving bells. But he had never experienced quite the view that the great bow ports of the *Seaview* offered.

Banks was a bachelor in his mid-thirties, but he seemed older to Crane and Nelson, who found him likable but extremely sober and serious, as if he were constantly worried about the shape the world was in.

He glanced anxiously now at the broad, transparent ports. "I can't help feeling uneasy," he said, "about whether or not those windows are going to hold. I can't imagine a plastic or glass that would keep out the tons and tons of water which are now above us."

Crane laughed. "There's never been a leak even around the joints. Actually it's neither plastic nor glass. We call it X-hardened Herculite. It's one of the Admiral's minor inventions."

"A major one, I'd say!" The geologist moved closer and peered out in fascination at the sea world illuminated by the lights. A large grouper fish drifted lazily by and peered in at them. In the distance Crane thought he saw the outline of a blue shark.

Admiral Nelson joined Banks. "Do you still feel we're likely to find some unusual things at Oil City?"

"The earthquake itself was most unexpected. This is about as unlikely a site as I can imagine.

In spite of the damage, it was quite a small quake. Just before we left, Madrid said they showed two-point-five on their scale. Algiers reported a reading of two-point-zero."

"It was big enough to wipe out Oil City Eighteen."

"At any rate," said Banks, "it shows there is still plenty we don't know about underwater geology."

"Which is hardly surprising. Men have been exploring the land surface of the earth for quite a few thousand years, and we don't know all about it yet. The bottom of the sea is more than twice as large, and we've been poking around it for only a couple of decades. In another thousand years we'll know something about it—maybe."

The helmsman called out over the intercom, "Depth, one hundred and thirty fathoms. Fifteen fathoms to bottom. Oil City Eighteen, dead ahead."

"Hold at fifteen above bottom," said Crane. "Reduce speed and prepare to stop."

The sonar operator spoke up. "There's a noise —something—on the detector." He switched it to the speaker, and a thunderous roaring filled the ship. He switched it off.

"That sounds like a tornado," said Banks. "What could make such a sound nine hundred feet under the ocean?"

"Tornado may not be a bad word for it," said Nelson. "I think we'll find it's the oil gusher. Oil and gas from the ruptured wells are creating a tremendous turbulence, and that's what we're hearing."

The fierce, angry sound struck them all with a sense of the mighty forces of nature that surrounded them. Banks reflected that each square foot of the transparent port in front of his face bore a pressure of over twenty-five tons from the weight of the water above them. He shuddered faintly and wondered why he hadn't stuck to the geology of desert prospecting, where water came in precious pints.

"There it is!" exclaimed Crane suddenly. He swung the searchlight beam through a small arc ahead of the *Seaview*. In the dim distance a boiling column a half-mile thick extended from the bed of the sea to invisible heights above them.

"Every well must have ruptured," said Nelson.

Boiling, frothing sea water curled and surged at the edge of the column, while its dark core of black crude oil seemed to stand motionless and terrible. Then, as the submarine approached slowly, the men could see that the thick, black column was actually several smaller columns that merged in the dark heights of the water above. They counted five individual columns, between which water seethed with bright froth in the light of the search beams.

No one spoke. It was a scene of terror, of nature's forces gone wild. To exert any control over that chaos seemed utterly beyond the ability of man.

"Swing the light down," said Admiral Nelson. "I want to see the houses and shops."

Dark hemispheres on the sea floor ringed the raging column of oil. These were the buildings where oilmen and their families had lived. Shops and warehouses and power stations were here, too. They were laid out in clusters, with streets marked between them. Passageways extended from each group of houses to the central building that served as a small center for shopping, entertainment, and visiting.

It was a miniature city on the floor of the sea.

But the lights that once brightened the streets and ringed the major centers were dead. The nuclear power plant, which had always blazed with light, was dark.

Nelson's eyes held on the darkened power plant. "Get a check on radioactivity," he requested Crane. "If the reactor has cracked open we'll never be able to get near the site."

Crane ordered the reading made. In a moment a crewman reported. "The count is normal," said Crane. "The reactor must be intact."

"Do you think anyone could still be alive in those houses?" asked Banks. "Some of them look as if they might not be damaged."

"We're here to find out," said Crane. "But I don't think we'll find survivors. The crew will be making a check for them while you find out what you can of the effects of the quake—and its cause."

"There's enough work in that assignment for a staff of ten for a year," said Banks.

"North American Oil might be willing to support such a study," said Nelson. "All of the oil companies would be willing to pay well to learn how to prevent a disaster like this."

The submarine continued its slow advance until it was over the clusters of houses. Crane directed the helmsman to maneuver to an open space near the powerhouse and descend to the floor of the sea.

"You said you'd worked at these depths before?" Crane asked Banks.

The geologist nodded. "I can take care of myself."

"I'm sure you can. I'll assign two crewmen to assist you in gathering data. They'll be equipped with photographic instruments and with picks, ropes, and baskets for collecting geological samples. Will you need anything else?"

"Not at present. Are we ready to go?"

Crane nodded. "Chief Petty Officer Jones will direct the search for possible survivors. The admiral—" Crane stopped and looked at Nelson —"I don't suppose the admiral could be kept from going out, regardless of the hazards."

Nelson smiled. "You're right, Captain. I'm at your disposal."

"You and I will make a general survey of the site to report to North American Oil and to the government. Let's go!"

The *Seaview* settled to the bottom with a gentle rocking motion. The helmsmen and the diving crew remained at their posts in the control room. The radio operator prepared to check out communication channels in the radio-equipped diving suits.

There were twelve in the exploring party. They entered the air lock and began donning the suits. As the door was dogged shut, Crane set the atmosphere controls to build up a mixture of helium and oxygen at a pressure of almost twenty-five times the normal atmospheric pressure. This would equalize the enormous pressure of the water outside.

Through years of experimentation, workers at the bottom of the sea had found there was no difficulty in facing such pressures if the atmosphere being breathed was equal in pressure to the outside water pressure. This means that there is no difference in pressure between the outside of the human body and the organs on the inside. But it was found that ordinary atmosphere, containing nitrogen, could not be used. Nitrogen, under pressure, produced effects almost like intoxication. So hydrogen was used in its place. Later, helium was found to be just as satisfactory and far safer, since a mixture of hydrogen and oxygen is highly explosive.

In the subsea atmosphere approximately 3 percent oxygen is used, instead of the 20 percent in the normal atmosphere. The exact composition of the deep sea atmosphere depends on the depth, and some mixtures use small amounts of other gases, too.

In the suits, the men waited patiently until a

buzzer announced the gas pressure in the chamber equaled the water pressure outside. They adjusted their masks and began breathing the gas mixture from their tanks.

Crane switched on his radio for a check. "Everybody on board? Okay. Let's go!"

He turned the handles and undogged the door leading to the open sea in the floor of the chamber. The water lapped at the edge of it, held back by the gas pressure in the room. Crane dropped through the opening. One by one, the others followed him.

Outside they grouped according to their assignments, but they remained together as they swam slowly along the street of undersea houses for a preliminary survey. They could see now that nearly all of the buildings were twisted or split open by the force of the quake. The search for survivors would not take long, Crane thought.

The thundering turbulence of the nearby oil gushers roared in their ears and seemed to hammer at their very bones. Crane recognized that very much more of this kind of buffeting would soon become unbearable.

They swam over the row of buildings nearest the oil field. Crane was about to order them to separate and begin their missions when a sudden cry came from Curley Jones, the chief petty officer.

"Captain!"

Crane had not been particularly aware of Curley's whereabouts. Now he flashed his light about. The beam caught Curley's figure swimming desperately toward them but receding at a steady, increasing rate.

"Curley! What is it? What's the matter with you?"

"The current!" gasped Curley. "There's a current over here. I can't fight it!"

"The vortex!" cried Nelson. "He's being sucked into the vortex of the oil gusher. It'll carry him to the top. He'll decompress and explode!"

It was like a whirlpool in reverse, Crane thought. "Fight it!" he thundered at Curley. Then he hurled himself toward the crewman who carried the spear gun which was always present to guard against predatory fish in unfamiliar waters. Crane seized the gun and swam to the man who carried Banks's gear. He looped one end of the thin nylon rope about the hook at the end of the spear. He looped the other end about his own wrist and aimed the spear above Curley's head.

His heart froze as he saw how far away Curley was. "Fight it!" he cried again. "I'm going to shoot this rope over your head. Grab it and hang on!"

The spear hissed through the water. The dragging rope slowed it and shortened its range. It arrowed above Curley—but not quite far enough out to reach him.

Desperately the seaman fought the current. His fingers reached for the spear and failed.

"Swim, Curley! Swim!" his companions screamed at him.

Then the current caught at the spear and sucked it closer. Curley kicked upward and his fingers closed over it.

"I've got it," he panted. "I've got it!"

Crane immediately felt the tug of the current as it dragged at Curley and himself. "Come on —all of you!" he cried. "Pull!"

The others swam close and seized the rope. Awkwardly they applied their efforts together and drew the struggling Curley out of the deadly grip of the current. He swam into their midst, panting and grateful.

"Maybe you'd better go back to the ship," Crane said.

"I'm okay, Captain. Just a little winded, that's all. Thanks, all of you. I'd be halfway to the top by now. Tornado is right! That thing will suck in everything that gets near it!"

"We should have expected this," said Crane. "All of you men be warned now. Keep your distance from that vortex. Let's go now and get this tour finished."

Crane and Nelson swam toward the power station. They could feel the constant drag of the current moving toward the oil field, and they had to exert themselves to swim against it. As they moved, Crane constantly checked the radiation meter strapped to his wrist. They found the power station building flooded through rents in its walls and ceilings, but miraculously the reactor had remained sealed.

"It's safe for the time being, anyway," said Nelson, "but there's no telling how long it will stay that way. This building ought to be resealed and pumped out as the first order of salvage."

Crane glanced upward at the gaping holes and slits in the dome. "I'm not sure I'd care for that assignment. It's going to take some real engineering to salvage this plant."

"Let's move on down to the shops and warehouses."

These buildings held all the machinery that had kept the oil field functioning, including the pumps that filled the submarine tankers which carried the crude oil to the refineries up on the surface.

As they were about to enter a flooded warehouse, Curley's voice again rang in their ears. "Captain—"

"*Now* what's he got himself into?" Crane muttered. He switched over to the general channel that would carry his voice to all the men. "This is the captain. What is it now, Curley?"

"We've found a survivor, Captain. The survey is complete. Just one survivor."

"Good work. What kind of condition is he in?"

"I'm not sure, Captain. I think you'd better come quick and look for yourself. We're in the last house on Avenue C."

"Curley, can't you take care of the situation?" Crane asked irritably.

"I really think you should come, Captain."

Seaman Jenkins, on Curley's team, joined in. "I agree, Captain. I think it's most urgent that you come."

Crane groaned. "All right. I guess I'll have to see what's so complicated that you able-bodied seamen can't take care of it. Admiral?" He glanced at Nelson.

"Right with you," said Nelson.

They approached the house Curley had indicated and saw that it was indeed intact. Almost the only one. They dipped into the U-shaped entrance lock and swam up into the entrance hall. The atmosphere in the house was still at full pressure. The men hoisted themselves out of the water and stood dripping. The room was lighted by the lanterns held by Curley and Jenkins.

"All right, what is it?" snapped Crane. "Where is the survivor?"

"In here," said Curley. He led the way to the next room.

For a moment Crane stared, not seeing what he was supposed to see. Then he recognized a crib, and lying within it a feebly squirming bundle. A baby's faint cry filled the room.

Crane blinked in astonishment and dismay. "Holy mackerel! How did a baby get down here in a sea city?"

"What's more important, if you'll pardon me," said Curley, "is how in the world do we get it out?"

2

THE BABY was clothed in a zippered sleeping suit that was like a small mummy bag. The temperature of the room was only a few degrees above freezing, but the infant looked comfortable in spite of the cold. Yet for at least two days it must have been in this frigid atmosphere and without food.

The question of how the baby got there was of secondary importance. The important question was how to get it to the warmth of the submarine and fed as quickly as possible.

Curley Jones had been exploring the room. Now he came up behind Crane with a piece of paper in his hand. "I guess this was left by the child's mother," he said.

Crane grasped the paper and read it aloud quickly.

"If anyone finds this, I hope it is in time to save my baby. The earthquake happened ten hours ago. I have been outside, and no one else is alive. My baby and I are alone. His father was in the machine shop when it happened. The central atmosphere plant is destroyed, and I've been able to find only a few suit bottles with gas. I know there's not enough for both of us for very long. There's no heat, but I've dressed him as warmly as possible. I've fed him. I've opened the available air bottles to trickle fresh air into the room as long as possible. I pray my baby will live until searchers come. I'm going outside now.

"P.S. His name is Gordon."

The note was unsigned.

Curley looked up with anguish in his eyes. "Outside—" he said slowly. He glanced to the ports that showed the sea outside at this nine-hundred-foot depth. "She just—"

"Yes," said Crane, "she sacrificed herself to save the baby's life. And she was right. The oxygen in here wouldn't have been enough for both of them. Now we've got to get the baby to the *Seaview* as quickly as possible."

"Any ideas, Captain?" said Curley.

"Yes. You and Jenkins go back and get a full suit with tanks. We'll inflate it and carry the baby in it. And while you're there tell Jamie to rig up a feeding bottle out of something and to get a warm bath ready. Also diapers and blankets."

"You bet!" said Curley. "We'll have Sea Baby as snug as a bug in a rug in no time."

Alone with the baby, Crane and Nelson waited silently, thinking of the mother who had been there for ten long hours, knowing she and the baby were the last ones alive. They thought of her decision to go out into the sea and leave the infant with all possible chance of survival.

Abruptly the water thrashed in the entrance lock and Curley popped up, with Jenkins close behind. They hoisted a suit and set of tanks behind them. Curley dragged the equipment close to the crib and crooned, "It's going to be all right, Sea Baby. We'll have you out of here before you know it."

"Gordon is the child's name," said Admiral Nelson.

"Uh-uh. Sea Baby, that's who he is," said Curley. "Sea Baby he's going to be."

"Never mind. Give a hand here," said Crane.

It was a difficult, twenty-minute task for the four men to get the small, protesting infant safely encased in the suit. They tied off the arms and legs and the lower part of the suit to keep them from getting in the way. Then they lowered the awkward bundle into the water and swam carefully with it to the submarine.

The whole ship had been alerted. When they reached the lock, Dr. Jamieson, the ship's doctor, had warm milk ready, and a makeshift nipple constructed from a sterilized rubber glove. Warm water was ready in a dishpan baby bath. Sheets had been cut to diaper size, and blankets and a heating pad were ready.

Jamieson stayed outside the lock so he wouldn't have to spend long hours in decompression, but he watched intently as Curley held the baby up to the window for his inspection. He directed the men to measure temperature and heartbeat and blood pressure with the instruments he had passed into the air lock.

Curley fed the baby a trickle of milk until Jamieson said it was enough. Then he laid out blankets and prepared the bath. Crane, Nelson, and Jenkins watched as the chief petty officer performed his tasks expertly.

"It comes easy after you've done five of your own," he explained.

Crane stepped to the air controls to start the tedious, thirty-six hour process of decompressing. But Dr. Jamieson's voice roared over the loudspeaker. "Captain! Don't do that!"

Crane turned in puzzlement. "What's wrong? We've got to get out of here."

"The baby," said Jamieson. "Do you realize it was probably born down here in a helium-oxygen atmosphere? It has never had nitrogen in its lungs, nor has it experienced normal, sea-level pressure."

Crane took his hand from the valves. "So what do we do? Are you trying to say that it will never

be possible to decompress Sea Baby?"

"I don't know," said Jamieson. There was despair in his voice. "I'm sure nobody in the world has ever faced this problem before. Who was foolish enough to let that woman go down there in the first place? I suggest we get in touch with Martin at the Institute. He knows more than all the rest of us put together regarding high-pressure atmospheres and decompression."

"All right," said Crane. "Have him contacted by radio, and see what he says. In the meantime, we'll put Sea Baby in the decompression chamber and hold it steady so the rest of us can get out of the lock."

Curley looked up in horror. "You can't put him in there all by himself and leave him! Who's going to take care of him?"

Crane grinned and stepped to the door of the decompression chamber and began to undog it. "Guess who," he said.

Hours later the giant nuclear submarine had surfaced and was racing at full speed for the

Guatemala Canal, from where it would speed up the California coast to Santa Barbara and home base. Dr. Martin had refused to take responsibility for Sea Baby unless he could examine him before decompression was attempted.

Banks and his group and the remainder of Curley's crew had come aboard and decompressed in a second lock long after Sea Baby had been brought aboard. After their thirty-six hours of decompression, Banks made his report.

"We circled the gusher area," he said, "and found no fissures or fault displacement. We will be able to plot the direction of the displacement wave from our photographs and plots. All in all, we did about everything possible in a preliminary survey. I'm going to recommend a full-scale study, of course."

Crane and Nelson agreed the expedition could be considered a success even though they had left early because of Sea Baby.

When the submarine reached the Institute base there was much excitement among the staff.

Sober marine geologists didn't ask Banks about fault structure or seismograph reports. They asked about Sea Baby.

Dr. Martin, the Institute's specialist in marine physiology, boarded the *Seaview* as soon as it docked. Crane knew it would be hours before Martin would have anything to tell them. The doctor didn't believe in preliminary reports. Crane left a skeleton crew, including technicians to watch the chamber. Curley was sweating out his own decompression now in one of the locks. Otherwise, the crew disembarked for the Institute buildings and home.

Halfway to the Administration Building, Crane spotted a small, dark-haired tornado emerging from the main entrance and whirling toward him.

"Cathy!"

Cathy Kinney rushed excitedly up to Lee Crane and began talking in a flood of words while he tried to slow down the almost unintelligible verbal torrent.

"Listen!" she exclaimed. "I've had the most

wonderful idea, and I don't want anyone else to think of it. I'm going to take care of Sea Baby."

"Now wait a minute!" Crane responded. "Nobody's going to take care of anybody. He's got folks somewhere. Grandparents, aunts, uncles— somebody. We'll have to find out who they are and turn him over to them."

"But if we don't find them, I'll do it."

"You haven't even seen him."

"But I'm going to!" She tugged at his arm and started for the quay. "Come on. I want to see him now."

"Say, I thought we had a date tonight. Besides, you can't. Martin's in the chamber."

"Oh, I can talk Martin out of his last Band-Aid. And our date can wait."

Reluctantly, but happily, Lee Crane hurried along beside the chattering Cathy. It was good to be back home again.

Dr. Martin scowled fiercely through the port of the decompression chamber as Lee and Cathy looked in. But he went on with his examination of the baby, who was lying on a small table.

"He's adorable!" said Cathy.

"He always needs a haircut," said Crane.

"He—he hasn't got any hair! Oh, I meant the baby, stupid!"

Dr. Martin switched on the intercom and grunted. "As far as I can see, this baby is perfectly normal and healthy. He has suffered no harm from the exposure, and I would swear he had never missed a meal. I think we can start decompression now, but *very* slowly, you understand. Not less than three weeks. I'm not yet certain of the point at which to introduce nitrogen into his atmosphere. I'll give you the rates and gas mixtures when I get to the lab. I'll go into decompression now. Who's going to attend the baby? Someone must be with him constantly."

"Chief Petty—" Crane began.

"I will," said Cathy.

"Look, I just got home," said Crane.

"And you don't bring a new baby with you every trip, either."

Crane began to regret the whole thing.

"I'll need you aboard within the hour," said Dr. Martin.

"I'll be there," Cathy promised.

Admiral Nelson had called a staff meeting for that afternoon to discuss the findings of the expedition and to plan their reports and further study. Crane had hoped that for once the admiral wouldn't be such an eager beaver and would put off the conference until the following day, at least. But he was resigned. He went to the meeting while Cathy prepared to attend Sea Baby.

Before Nelson opened the meeting in the conference room of the Institute, his staff assistant, Barker, asked for the floor.

"Before you discuss your expedition, Admiral, I think you and everyone else might be interested in a summary of events of the past three weeks which have been reported to the Institute. This has been a period quite unlike any other in the history of deep-sea exploitation."

"Go ahead," said Nelson. "Bring us up to date."

"Three weeks ago the Hawaiian Fish Farm,

which accounts for twenty percent of our controlled fishing, was invaded by some species of killer fish entirely new to our biologists. The commercial species were virtually wiped out— and the invader is useless as a food fish.

"Event number two: Under the Japanese continental shelf a mine cave-in wiped out an entire shift of mine workers and destroyed the workings. Then there occurred the incident which you investigated at Oil City.

"Finally: Less than an hour ago, word was received that the natural gas fields in the North Sea, which supply nearly all of England, were hit by a quake and ruptured. The escaping gas caught fire, perhaps from lightning, and hundreds of square miles of the North Sea are one enormous flare.

"This has been a month of unprecedented marine disasters."

Barker sat down. Admiral Nelson made no comment beyond a dissatisfied grunt. Crane watched him out of the corner of his eye as Banks then reported his results. Nelson finally dismissed the meeting with a curious lack of interest in the proceedings.

Afterward, he cornered Crane and led him off to the big chart room. "What do you make of these things Barker reported?"

"I don't know," said Crane. "I guess there's nothing to make of them except that, like Oil City Eighteen, they need some thorough investigation and study to keep them from repeating."

"Doesn't it strike you as curious that so much disaster should happen all at once?"

"Why? A hurricane hits Florida while a typhoon strikes the Philippines, and an earthquake levels some town in the Near East, and a crop failure occurs in Russia. These things happen all the time."

"That's just it," said Nelson. "They happen all the time on the surface. But when, in the last twenty years, has something like this happened in the sea?"

"I don't know," said Crane, "but we haven't been in the sea long enough to attach any peculiar significance to things like this. Maybe hundreds of earthquakes hit the African Shelf and the North Sea before we had installations there. We didn't know of such things until we put some installations down there."

"In twenty years," Nelson insisted. "We've had several score installations there for over half that time. How many have experienced such destruction as has occurred in this three-week period?"

Crane could recall only one open-pit mining operation that had been hit by any real disaster. The sea had been quiet and had treated man well as long as Crane could remember. "Just what are you trying to say?" he asked at last.

"I'm trying to say that what's happened is so unusual that I think there must be some common factor involved. Some common agent."

Crane stared. "How could there be a connection between killer fish in Hawaii and broken gas lines in the North Sea?"

"Whoever ruptured the gas lines could have planted the fish."

"You're talking about an *enemy!*"

Nelson nodded slowly. "Yes, I guess I am."

"Who? The world is at peace. There is reasonable political stability almost everywhere."

"Not if these disasters are happening by intention."

"But we don't know that. And, besides—these were *earthquakes*."

"Perhaps," said Nelson. "Keep it under your hat for a few days. Do some thinking. Maybe the *Seaview* will be going out again sooner than we think."

Crane felt too dazed to do any thinking as he left the Institute. It was just too much to believe that human agency was involved in the Oil City disaster, for example. In fact, the more he thought about Nelson's words, the more crazy they seemed. No earthquake like that could have been produced artificially. On the other hand, even Banks had said the seabed didn't look as if an earthquake had taken place there.

Crane gave it up and went home. He found Cathy there, waiting for him.

"You're not going down to the *Seaview?*" he asked.

"I've been down and talked fussbudget Martin out of a few hours. The baby is asleep, and I won't go down until evening. I found some interesting things down there, however, and I wanted you to see them." She held up some baby clothing.

"They're the things Sea Baby was wearing when we found him."

"I know. Look at this and tell me where you ever saw anything like it before."

"Look at what?"

Cathy was holding the zippered suit. She moved the fastener slowly up and down.

"It's a zipper," said Crane. "You know—zip, and it's shut."

"Look at it." Cathy held it toward him.

He looked more closely. "It's one of those plastic types. I hadn't noticed that before."

"Did you ever see a plastic one that closed like that?"

To please her, he looked more closely. Then, suddenly, he stared hard. Two ribbed edges of plastic touched each other on perfectly flat surfaces as the fastener moved. There were no projections, teeth, or interlocking devices of any kind. But after they had been zipped up, the two flat surfaces couldn't be pulled apart, no matter how hard he tried.

"I'll be darned," Crane said. "That really is a new kind. Wonder where it was made."

"I found out something else that's interesting, too," said Cathy. "You mentioned that Sea Baby would have folks to claim him, so I looked up the records of Oil City Eighteen to find out who his parents were."

"So you won't have to take care of him, after all," said Crane in relief.

"So I found out that the occupants of Oil City Eighteen were all men. There were no families there. Sea Baby's mother wasn't there."

"That's crazy! We found the note from her. I've still got it. Besides, if that were true, how *did* the baby get there? No oil-town bachelor roughneck would be smuggling a baby down there!"

"That's *your* problem. I'm just telling you what

the records say. The official records. Now put
that with this funny-looking zipper thing and see
what you can figure out!"

Lee Crane found it hard to sleep that night.
So many unexplained happenings kept marching
through his consciousness shouting for answers
he didn't have. What had started out as a perfectly normal expedition to investigate a tragic
but natural occurrence at Oil City Eighteen had
begun a nightmare of puzzles.

Obviously there was something wrong with
the official records that said Sea Baby's mother
was not there at the time of the earthquake. And,
equally as obvious, Admiral Nelson was having
pipe dreams when he suggested there could be
a connection between the fish farm disaster in
Hawaii and the ruptured, flaming gas wells in
the North Sea.

What were the answers to these problems? In
addition, who were Sea Baby's parents, and how
was anyone going to find out?

The questions tumbled in his mind until he

sat up and looked at the clock and saw it was three A.M. He wondered why the alarm had gone off at that time. Then he realized it wasn't the alarm. It was the telephone. He muttered sleepily and irritably to himself and got up to answer it. Admiral Nelson was calling.

"There's been another one," said the admiral. "The Corbazzi Mines, about five hundred miles north of Oil City Eighteen. A big cave-in, but the city is only partly damaged, and they think there may be survivors. The *Seaview* leaves in an hour!"

"Wait a minute!" yelled Crane. "Supplies aren't on board. Cathy and Sea Baby are there in the decompression chamber. The crew is scattered all over town."

"Supplies are being loaded now. I've explained things to Cathy. She'll be delighted to take a trip aboard with us. The crew is being called by my staff now. All the *Seaview* needs is a skipper. Are you her captain or not?"

"Coming," said Crane. "I'll be there in twenty minutes."

3   The Magnetic Field

THE RECREATION hall of the mine village of Corbazzi was a dome-covered building the size of a football field. Normally it was warmed by radiant floor and walls, and light panels over the great dome made it daylight bright.

But the power was gone. The quake had severed the distribution cables and shorted the generators. The hall was icy cold, and dark except for a hundred bobbing flashlights and a few emergency battery-powered floodlights.

A couple of hundred survivors huddled in small, tight groups, silent or whispering softly in the shock that followed disaster. Some sat on the cold floor, blankets and coats wrapped about them. But there were few such coverings;

the sea cities depended on nuclear-powered electricity for warmth and light.

The injured were grouped at one end. Two of the mine doctors and their four nurses moved quietly among them, administering sedatives and antibiotics. Two emergency operations had already been performed under the battery-powered floodlights. One more was in progress.

The cries of children were the loudest sound in the hall. Only those over a year old were permitted in the sea cities, but there were a score of these and they were frightened, cold, and hungry.

Captain Lee Crane and Admiral Harriman Nelson stood in the entrance hall, moisture draining from their suits, as they looked at the scene of refuge. They opened their faceplates and breathed the air of the hall. It was obvious that the oxygen in the hall was getting low.

"Air regeneration is out," said Crane.

"We can hook up the *Seaview's* equipment," said Nelson. "It will tide things over until we get some chambers to take these people up."

"Right. I'll have cables laid from our generators, too, in order to warm up this place and give some light." Crane switched on his radio and detailed his commands to the officers aboard the submarine. He also ordered a radio message to the United Nations offices requesting immediate assistance from all nations with decompression chambers to evacuate the survivors.

As he finished, two men broke away from a group at the near end of the hall and came rapidly forward. One of them extended a hand in hearty welcome.

"You men must be Captain Crane and Admiral Nelson," he said. "I'm Adam Cox, general manager of Corbazzi, and this is my mine superintendent, George Mahos."

"We're glad to know you," said Crane. "I'm the captain, and this is Admiral Nelson. We were at home base when word of the quake came. We were at Oil City Eighteen just a few days ago."

"Ah, yes," said Cox. "We heard of the misfortune of those poor people, never thinking that we would soon be in the same situation. But tell me, what are your plans, and what can we do to help? As you have seen up above, two company vessels have arrived some time ago, and their decompression chambers are already in use. Forty of our people, mostly the injured, are on the way up in them."

"We're hooking up air and electricity from the *Seaview* right now," said Crane. "We've radioed for additional chambers. What about your own transport chambers? Are they serviceable?"

"My men are getting two ready now. The third was damaged beyond repair."

"What's their capacity?" asked Nelson.

"Twenty persons each."

"So altogether, using the chambers above, plus these two, you can get eighty people out of here almost immediately?"

"Almost. The injured, of course, are going first. They take more room."

"What about the men in the mine?" asked Crane. "Are there any survivors who can be brought out?"

"We know that at least ten are still alive in there," said Cox sadly. "But the mouth of the mine is entirely collapsed; all of our staging platform is gone. If we could get a Mine Charley and some bracing to the mouth, we might be able to get in. But platforms, cables, cranes—everything was swept away."

"What's a Mine Charley?" asked Crane.

"It's our basic excavating machine for underwater mining. It has a dry-atmosphere cab for the operator, with powered manipulators for excavating and blasting."

"What about drilling from above to reach the survivors?" said Crane.

"No time. The men's air will run out long before we could reach them. The only hope is getting through the cave-in, but we can see no way to get a Mine Charley into position. Hand digging would be hopelessly slow."

"All right," said Crane, "let's suspend a Mine Charley from the *Seaview* and jockey it into position in front of the mine. We'll hold it there until your operator is able to dig himself a new

working ledge or get started into the mine itself.
Will that work?"

Cox and the mine superintendent looked at
each other. The anguish on their faces washed
away in a moment's sudden hope as they considered the possibility.

"Could you guide your submarine that pre-
cisely?" asked Cox. "It's so big—"

"It won't be easy—sort of like threading a
needle with a bulldozer," said Crane, "but we
can try. We've got to try, if that's the only possible way of reaching those men."

"What about the air and the electric cables?"
asked Mahos. "The air in here is very bad. I
don't think it can wait until the mine operation
is completed."

"We'll do it all at the same time," said Crane.
"You people scrape up all the large-gauge air
conduit in the place, and we'll hook up to the
Seaview's regenerators while we're holding a
Mine Charley in place."

The sea swarmed with Seaview's crewmen and
with mine rescue workers. They combined in

work teams under the overall direction of Curley Jones and Mine Superintendent Mahos. Two thousand feet of air conduit were laid between the recreation hall and the mine. Suspension cables were threaded from winches out through ports in the bottom of the submarine to attach to the Mine Charley. This machine was made ready, and the operator took his place while the *Seaview* jockeyed into position above it and the cables were laid.

Slowly the immense vessel lifted the machine and carried it to the almost vertical cliff face into which it must bore. Lieutenant Handley, at the helm of the *Seaview,* felt beads of sweat on his face as he attempted to bring the submarine into position. A television camera with floodlights mounted on the Mine Charley showed him his goal. The operator in the mining machine guided him by voice because it was almost impossible to tell where the mine opening once was. The mouth of it was nearly obliterated by the cave-in and the slide that followed.

The *Seaview* cleared the top of the cliff, which

formed the continental shelf, by fifty feet. The Mine Charley swayed at the end of the cables almost three hundred feet below. The smallest motion of the submarine swung the machine through a wide arc.

"We're coming in too fast!" the operator exclaimed. "We're going to hit!"

Handley swiftly reversed the propellers of the *Seaview* and brought the submarine to a halt. Currents in the water tugged at the submarine and the Mine Charley and moved them down the cliff face.

"I'll try it again," said Handley. "I think I've got it now. You're going to have to hit and dig in as soon as we touch, and I've got to head into the current."

"Right. Let's go, sailor boy!"

Lieutenant Handley pursed his lips and reminded himself to take that up with the miner at a later time.

Even while the agonizing maneuver was going on, the work crew was attaching the air conduit to the regenerators of the submarine to be-

gin restoring the oxygen of the recreation hall.
At the same time, they laid heavy electrical cables
to carry power for heat and light.

Admiral Nelson stood on the edge of the cliff
and watched the *Seaview* move up-current above
the cliff face once more. Scarcely moving, it hov-
ered in the water above him. In his phones he
could hear the exchange of conversation between
Handley and the miner.

"Another foot," the miner said. "Easy does
it . . . there!"

Below Nelson, in the searchlight beam, a sudden cloud of mud burst out into the water as the
great fans of the Mine Charley dug in and began to spit back the mud and debris that had
closed the mine. The cloud obscured the swimming miners who were bringing up sections of
metal bracing attached to floats to shield the
opening from further collapse as the machine
burrowed into it.

After twenty minutes the Mine Charley operator had cleared a ledge sufficient to support
his machine so that the cables from the *Seaview*

could safely be cast off.

During the operation Captain Crane had remained at the hall with Dr. Banks to interview the miners about the earthquake.

Underwater mining had become at least as safe as dry-land mining, and none of the miners had ever experienced a mine disaster before. They were shocked and numbed by it. But their reactions varied. Some were defiant; they boasted that they would be willing to go back into the mine right now.

Others were like the young miner with a wife and two small children in the hall. He shook his head and said, "I'll never come back. I thought this was a big adventure, but I found out different. I was in my Charley on the platform when it happened. I'd just come out for some repairs. If something hadn't gone wrong with the Charley, I'd have been in there now with those other guys. The mud and rock came sliding down the cliff and buried my Charley. The whole platform collapsed, and all I could do was grab my emergency helmet and blow the cockpit door. I thought I'd never get through the mudslide, but I managed to make it up to the edge of the shelf with nothing more than a broken arm. I'm lucky."

Another miner, an older man who'd spent half his life in dry-land mines, spoke up. "That's right! I thought the pay down here would help me retire in another five years. But they couldn't pay me enough to come back again.

"What I'd like to know is why that big submarine didn't come and help us? They must have felt the quake and known we were in trouble. But they just disappeared."

"What big submarine?" asked Crane. "You don't mean our *Seaview?*"

"Of course not. This one was three times as big as yours. Three times as long and three times as big around. Isn't that right?" he asked the crowd that hunched near them. The other men nodded.

"All of us who were outside saw it," said

another miner. "It passed over the village about ten minutes before the quake. But it never came back."

"It must have been a transport sub," said Crane, "off course and with a sonar out of kilter. I suppose it looked pretty big, but I guess you know there's no such boat registered anywhere in the world."

"We're not exaggerating," said the second miner. "It was that big. We all talked about it afterward; it wasn't fifty feet over our heads."

Crane left the subject. He didn't believe the report of the size of the submarine, of course. But the fact that there was any submarine at all was puzzling. He'd have to check the world traffic patterns for that day.

Banks continued his interviews. There was little enough he could learn, however. At just fifty minutes before the day shift was to go off, the miners all heard a "buzzing, rumbling noise that got louder and louder until it seemed to be right in the ground under our feet." Then the shelf began to rock and sway, and the great chunk of cliff face slid down and buried the mine.

Banks was interested in the "buzzing, rumbling noise," but they could tell him no more about it. Pandemonium had struck. Cox and Mahos had ordered everyone into the recreation hall, which was miraculously undamaged. Then they had begun rescue operations while sending out calls for help to the surface.

A crew of three *Seaview* scientist-technicians working with Banks made a survey of the machinery and equipment of the mine company. During the afternoon, they called Captain Crane and Admiral Nelson to observe a peculiarity.

"Everything's magnetized!" said Thompson, leader of the group. He pointed to the meter they had set up. "Steel objects are saturated. And there seems to be a magnetic field present even in normally non-magnetic materials. It almost seems to be in the very substance of the continental shelf."

Nelson glanced at the magnetometer thoughtfully. "How about Oil City Eighteen? Did you notice anything like that down there?"

"No, but it could have been there."

Nelson turned to Crane. "I think it's very important to know. How about sending a minisub to find out?"

"Sure—if you think it's worth the trip," said Crane.

"I do. Very much so."

Crane knew what the admiral was thinking. The common factor. Would this inexplicable magnetism be one? Crane switched on his radio and ordered Lieutenant Matthews, chief crewman of the minisub, to take the little vessel back to Oil City Eighteen to check for the magnetic phenomenon.

"Let's also ask the British Navy to make the same check at the North Sea disaster sites," said Nelson.

Slowly the sense of shock wore off, and the people of Corbazzi realized they could pick up the threads of their lives again. Some of them would stay with the sea. Some of them would leave it forever.

By midnight the Mine Charley had reached the pocket of survivors in the mine. Two had died from injuries, but the rest were alive.

Cathy Kinney divided her time between tending Sea Baby and assisting in caring for the injured. Crane and Nelson set up their headquarters in the pressure rooms adjacent to the lock. This was a portion of the submarine that could be pressurized to match the sea pressure during long periods of outside work. It made it unnecessary for the men to decompress and allowed them to use the submarine for a living and working headquarters.

Near morning a radio message came from Lieutenant Matthews: "Heavy magnetization in all steel in Oil City Eighteen."

They were at breakfast when the British Navy reported. "Peculiar intense magnetism in all piping and other metal objects in North Sea gas field. Additional data will be welcomed."

"It sure will," said Crane. "So now you have something common to three separate disaster sites. What next?"

"I'm thinking of the uncommon event that occurred here," said Nelson slowly. "The mysterious submarine which the miners described."

"We know it couldn't have been anything such
as they described," said Crane. "It could have
been one of a hundred things, a cloud of mud
jarred loose by the quake—"

"They said it was ten minutes *before* the
quake."

"Maybe a preliminary temblor hit somewhere
else first and sent a cloud of sediment through
the water. Maybe it was a whale."

"Out here?"

"It is far more likely that it was a whale than
a submarine of the size they gave."

"A whale three times as big as the *Seaview?*"

"Well, we know there's no such submarine on
record."

"Maybe there is now," said Nelson softly. "I
think maybe there's a pretty good chance there
is now."

4

Pursuit

ADMIRAL NELSON did not know the possible significance of the unexplained magnetism. Neither did any of his staff or crew. But Captain Crane had to admit that here, certainly, was a factor common to the three disasters. A tremendous magnetic field must have been present at some time to induce such magnetism. Did it mean that such a field accompanied the disaster, or was somehow connected with the cause of it?

Whatever it meant, a means had to be found to detect any future occurrence of such a field. This did not appear difficult to Nelson. He thought it possible to design a system of magnetic beacons to be placed on the sea bottom throughout the world. From these a sensitive magnetic detector could observe any marked disturbance in the normal magnetic patterns between beacons.

Nelson locked himself in a small private room of the pressure chamber to design such a beacon system and detector. After two days of incessant drawing and computing he emerged, blear-eyed and unshaven, with the design he was certain would accomplish his purpose.

By tight-beam, coded radio he sent the information to the Institute and ordered his technicians to begin production immediately of a hundred of the beacons. Then, by the secret code assigned to him, he contacted US Naval Headquarters regarding their placement.

The Navy agreed to plant the beacons. Within a week the first ones were ready. As fast as the simple devices came off the production line they were flown to submarine bases and dropped at strategic spots on the continental shelves around the world.

The whole operation was given a Top Secret rating.

At the end of the week rescue work at Corbazzi was nearly complete, and company crews had arrived for salvage and reconstruction. The *Seaview* became ready once more to move; all air and power lines were disconnected and the mine village became independent.

Sea Baby was still a problem. He was progressing well and had undergone partial decompression. Cathy was in daily communication with Dr. Martin. Dr. Jamieson verified the baby's condition.

Admiral Nelson considered it imperative that the *Seaview* undertake its magnetic patrol at once, which meant that Cathy and the baby had to remain at sea for at least another two weeks of decompression. At the end of that time they could be released at some seaport and flown back to Santa Barbara.

"I don't see what the problem is," said Cathy. "I *like* it here."

"The problem is that this time we don't know just what the hazards are—whether we'll run into natural disasters or man-made obstacles, or what," said Lee Crane. "We'll be fishing for something we're not even sure exists—but which may be very dangerous if it does exist."

"You mean the source of the mysterious magnetic field?"

"Yes."

"Sea Baby was born among such dangers, and I've lived with them before," said Cathy. "You haven't mentioned any problem yet."

Admiral Nelson considered it important enough to begin the survey at once that he agreed that Cathy and Sea Baby should stay. The *Seaview* put in at Gibraltar for supplies. Then it began a long, straight course across the Atlantic toward the Labrador coast, from where it would turn about and strike for Scotland, crisscrossing the ocean in long zigzags that would take it eventually to Cape Horn and the Cape of Good Hope. They would be at sea for months if the entire patrol were completed.

The *Seaview* sailed on the surface until she was beyond the continental shelf and over the deeps. Suddenly Cathy began to realize that she would be confined to the round steel walls of the decompression chamber for a full two weeks with nothing to see. She called Lee Crane on the phone. "How would *you* like to be in solitary confinement and not be able to see anything outside during the whole trip?"

"You want us to stop the boat and let you off? This was your idea, you know."

"With all the high-class electronic brainpower aboard this ship you could at least rig up a television set to the bow ports."

"Woman, don't you think the men of this ship have any work?"

"I'll bet the admiral would find a way to get it done."

That was the last thing in the world Crane wanted; Nelson was testy enough over the problems with his magnetic field recorders. "I'll see what some of the boys can do," Crane promised.

"I knew you would!" said Cathy.

"I know you knew I would," said Crane. "You know perfectly well the admiral would throw me overboard if you started heckling him now about something like that."

The following day the television set was installed. As Cathy had said, there was some high-class electronic brainpower aboard, and it didn't take them long to rig up the camera by the bow ports and put a receiver in the decompression chamber so she could see outside.

On a chart she followed their course. Experimenting with his magnetic detectors, Admiral Nelson ordered the *Seaview* to sail at all depths, from surface to the sea's bottom. Over the North Atlantic they dipped near the bottom, almost to the peaks of the rugged mounts between the Biscay Abyssal Plain and the Mid-Atlantic Range. Cathy watched the changing view on her private television screen.

In the thickly populated surface layers of the sea she recognized familiar forms of dolphins, groupers, amberjacks, sharks, and dozens of other fish she had learned to know. Below, in

the depths that were measured in thousands of feet, an eerie world of perpetual night surrounded the ship. But Cathy knew it was far from lifeless. Dozens of species of fish lazed by the ports of the submarine, carrying their own lights with them. When the searchlights of the ship were turned off, some sections of the sea became glowing fairylands. Ghostly, phosphorescent clouds of living creatures drifted by. Fish with glowing stalks probed the ports as if with miniature flashlights. Others sped by with luminous spots glowing on the sides of their bodies like the lighted portholes of strange little ships of the deep.

In mid-Atlantic the submarine rose to clear the mountainous heights of the Mid-Atlantic Range, the longest mountain range on the earth. Then it surfaced until it was over the Mid-Ocean Canyon, lying east of the Grand Banks and the coast of Newfoundland. Here, the *Seaview* dipped to the bottom again, and Cathy watched the little burrows and mounds on the sea floor, created by mysterious, unnamed creatures that built their tunnels and houses where no surface creature could survive.

Not until they neared the Labrador coast and turned back toward Scotland was Nelson completely satisfied with his instruments. By that time several dozen of the magnetic beacons had been planted, most of them on the continental shelves of the Atlantic, and their steady magnetic field was being accurately recorded in the *Seaview*.

The crossing to Scotland was uneventful. The submarine wove its way west again on a more southerly course to the Nova Scotia region, then eastward once more, where they put in at Cherbourg, France for a couple of days of rest and some supplies.

They touched America near the New England coast and shuttled back toward the coast of Spain. It was when they had reached the longitude of the Madeira Islands that the alarm connected to the magnetic detector rang with shrill warning. A tremendous upset in the existing magnetic field had been recorded. The detector operator checked his indicators and watched intently as the automatic magnetic tracker locked on the source of that disturbance, just as a radar beam locks on an enemy aircraft.

The operator made minor adjustments and checked the computer record that was slowly unwinding. "It's locked on!" he reported finally. "It's locked on to something. Range, two hundred and ten miles. Bearing, one hundred and thirty-four degrees."

"Put us on autopilot with input from the tracker," Crane ordered.

Nelson was intent on the chart nearby. He beckoned to Crane and traced a straight line with his finger to the location of the disturbance.

"Look what's nearby," he said.

"Anatolia Copper!" Crane exclaimed. "I wonder—" He called to the radio room. "Contact Anatolia Copper!"

"What message, sir?"

"The *Seaview* wishes a check contact."

They waited. Crane and Nelson stared at the spot on the map of the undersea region south-west of Gibraltar. Crane tried to remember what he knew of the region. He knew it was the world's largest undersea copper development.

The intercom came to life. "I'm sorry, sir. I can't raise the Anatolia Copper station. There is no transmission on their frequency, and they do not answer my call."

"Thanks," said Crane heavily.

"Shall I try again?"

"Not now. Later, perhaps."

Admiral Nelson stared at the chart, his jaws tensed. Crane knew they were thinking the same thing. Another Oil City. Another Corbazzi.

"Should we—" Crane began.

"No," said Nelson. "We've got to track that thing, whatever it is. If we let it go, how many more Oil Cities or Corbazzi Mines may there be? I'll radio Washington and the UN to get submarines and chambers to Anatolia Copper as soon as possible. But keep *Seaview* on course!"

Crane stood behind the tracker operator and watched the steady indication. The disturbance itself was gone, but they were tracking something enormous in size and magnetic in nature. Crane thought of the words of the Corbazzi miners: "three times as big as the *Seaview!*"

Where could such a ship come from—if it were actually a ship? And if it were responsible for the disasters, how were they accomplished? Here was a force that shook the earth with the thunder of earthquakes. The *Seaview* itself couldn't create such a monstrous force.

The whole situation seemed utterly impossible. But it was there.

The *Seaview* was running at top underwater speed now. Crane ordered her cautiously raised to the surface to increase speed, but he watched carefully that they didn't lose their target. Surfacing seemed to make no difference. The detector remained locked on the distant mysterious object, and the range was slowly decreasing.

Satisfied that the ship and its equipment were functioning properly, Crane went below to see Cathy. She had sensed something unusual from the sudden surfacing of the ship, but she had refrained from disturbing Crane at his duties.

She looked at him now through the thick port of the decompression chamber while her voice came over the intercom. "What will happen when we catch them?"

Crane shook his head. "That's what worries me. All I can think of is to follow until they make port somewhere. I don't know if the admiral has something up his sleeve or not."

"Would we attack?"

"I don't see how we can—unless they attack us first."

"We wouldn't have much of a chance if they got a first strike with a nuclear torpedo, would we?"

"We're not exactly defenseless, but it would be rough. I wish you weren't here."

Cathy smiled through the glass. "I'm glad I am. It's going to be all right."

Crane returned her smile. "I may not be able to get down again before we make contact."

She blew him a kiss. He hurried up the ladder to the control room.

During the succeeding hours Crane stood

in the control room, his eyes seldom moving from the detector instruments or the course indicator. Nelson joined him after getting off the message for help for Anatolia Copper.

Their target moved toward the African coast, then turned southwestward to parallel it for a considerable distance. When the *Seaview* had closed to within twenty miles, the target suddenly headed directly for the coast.

"It looks as if it's heading for port," said Crane. "But that section of the coast is completely barren."

"It would be surfacing if it were going to make port," said Nelson. "But it's still at nine hundred feet. It will ram the continental shelf. It's got to stop or rise soon. Let's go down and follow at the same depth."

Crane gave the necessary diving orders.

The target showed no sign of slowing. Crane and Nelson watched for some unexpected maneuver, but the target continued on to a line where the charts said the continental shelf began—and crossed it.

"The chart's wrong," said Nelson. "I wonder where the shelf line is, anyway."

"There's something awfully wrong here," said Crane. "I'm going to take it easy." He signaled his crewmen. "Reduce speed—ten knots."

"The target's making twenty," said Nelson.

"He knows where he's going. I don't."

The sonar alarm suddenly sounded, and the operator called out, "Obstacle ahead! Shelf line, one thousand yards."

"Reduce speed!" Crane ordered. "Three knots."

He and Nelson hurried to the bow ports in the observation room and turned on the search-light beams. "This is crazy!" Crane muttered.

Silently they watched as the *Seaview* edged closer to the continental shelf. The magnetic detector still indicated that the target had vanished like a wraith beyond it.

"We're chasing ghosts," the detector operator said.

Crane swung the searchlights about. "There it is," said Nelson. They caught a glimpse of shadowy mountain walls ahead of them.

"And our target just went right on through it. Have we been chasing some kind of electronic freak in our own instruments?" said Crane. "We—" He stopped. His breath sucked in with a hoarse gasp. "Look! Look ahead!"

"Where? What are you—"

Then Nelson became silent with disbelief. The cliff ahead was not a flat wall. It sloped inward and downward, forming a giant overhang, and straight ahead there was emptiness.

"A cavern!" exclaimed Crane. "It must be a mile wide. Sonar! Get our distance on all sides."

The sonar operator manipulated his instruments and called out the readings. "Fifteen hundred and fifty feet on the right. Thirty-three hundred and eighty on the left. Nineteen hundred on the bottom."

"It *is* a mile wide," breathed Crane. "How far ahead?"

"Forty-three hundred feet."

"Continue to advance slowly," Crane ordered. To Nelson he said, "This must be where our target disappeared. How far can such a cavern go? And *where* does it go?"

"We're not sure what we're chasing yet," said Nelson. "I think we'd better proceed only as far as the *Seaview* has room to turn around. If the cavern becomes too small for that we'll send the minisub."

"Right," said Crane.

Grottoes, shallow caverns, and small caves pocketed the edges of the continental shelves the world over. But never had the crewmen of the *Seaview* seen anything like this huge underwater cavern. The magnetic detector indicated their target was still ahead of them. It was going deeper, too, showing that the cavern descended to still greater depths.

Both Crane and Nelson were concerned about taking the ship into such a position. But they watched the sonar readings closely, and there was no sign of the cavern becoming narrower. They advanced a mile. Then two, and three. Suddenly the searchlights showed the cavern branched into equal arms leading right and left.

Crane checked the detector. "The target seems to be to the right."

In response to his command, the submarine turned slowly. Somewhere ahead, their target was very close. The detector showed a range of less than a mile. But the direction seemed erratic. Sometimes it was ahead. Sometimes it was directly at their left—through the rock walls of the cavern.

Nelson watched the erratic indication for long minutes. Then he understood. "We goofed," he said. "Our target's in the other branch."

"Maybe they come together somewhere ahead."

"It would be hopeless to count on that. Let's turn around."

Crane checked the current sonar readings. The ship seemed to have entered a huge pool. The walls were more than a half mile away on either side. But ahead there was a continuous echo now. There was no outlet ahead of them.

"It looks as if we've got to turn around whether we want to or not," said Crane.

The detector operator gave a sudden startled exclamation. "Captain! Admiral! The target—it's moving around. It's directly behind us now and closing fast!"

"Full rudder left!" ordered Crane.

Then, from out of the very space in the submarine, as if the hull plates themselves were vibrating with the tones of a threshing voice, there came the words: "Men of the *Seaview!* Do not run. If you try to escape, you will be destroyed. Stop your ship and rise to the surface two hundred feet above you!"

5

City of the Sea Kings

IN THE *Seaview* men stared at one another. They knew that the threatening voice which had rung out in every corner of the ship had no source within it. Some speaker in the sea beyond had the power to project the voice into the entire submarine.

Crane hesitated, instinctively glancing above him. The *Seaview* had nearly completed its turn. They were almost in a position to attack. But attack of any kind would be suicide in this cavern. A torpedo blast would destroy both ships.

Certainly the crew of the other ship did not dare fire, either. The *Seaview* could make a run for it if they could swing past the other vessel in the wide channel.

Crane watched the slowly turning gyrocompass. "Straight ahead!" he commanded. "Quarter speed. Keep to the right of the target!"

The target could be seen now. Through the bow ports, in the beams of the searchlights, a vast shadow lay in the depths ahead—a shadow of a vessel of impossible size. Crane felt as if a cold breath touched the back of his neck as they drew abreast of it.

The silence in the *Seaview* was suddenly broken again by the thunderous voice from the sea. "Men of the *Seaview*. You have been warned!"

The submarine began to shake with a furious vibration that penetrated every plate and girder. It tore wildly at the whole ship. The men were thrown to the floor.

As suddenly as it had begun, the terrible vibration ceased. Crane leaped to his feet and switched the intercom to general alarm. "Emergency check!" he commanded. "Reactor first, then all systems!"

Inch by inch the vessel would be combed for any damage to its structure or machinery.

Then the voice spoke again. "Men of the *Seaview,* you have been warned. Surface now!"

"I guess we'd better play it their way," said Nelson grimly.

"What in the world do they mean by 'surface'?" said Crane. "We're at eleven hundred feet, and they said to surface two hundred feet up."

"I don't know. Let's go up two hundred and see what's there."

One by one the reports came back from the inspection groups. "No damage." Crane knew finally that he still had a serviceable ship.

He gave orders to rise slowly by carefully pumping ballast. No one spoke as the reading of the depth gauge slowly decreased. The throbbing of the pumps and the hum of idling turbines were the only sounds.

Crane switched on the electronic periscope as the instruments told him the eye of the tube broke the two-hundred-foot limit. Instantly the periscope screen lit up an unbelievable sight.

The seamen gasped. Crane moved to the

screen as if he were hypnotized.

"A city!" he exclaimed. "A city in a cavern under the sea!"

For a moment it seemed as if they were no longer in the cavern. Over the city was a luminous sky as bright as day. Then it became apparent that the sky was a glowing cavern roof two or three hundred feet high.

The *Seaview* was floating in an undersea harbor a quarter of a mile from the city. Crane swung the periscope around. The far depths of the cavern could not be seen because of intervening buildings, but the men had the impression the cavern must extend three or four miles. Hundreds of buildings lined narrow streets.

Crane glanced at the pressure gauge that told the outside air pressure. "Nine hundred feet," he said. "The entire cavern is pressurized for nine hundred feet of water depth. Look—there's a crowd of people collecting on the dock."

What people were these? What nation had built such a fantastic submarine base as this? No one in the *Seaview* had any answers.

The people on the dock were dressed in indistinguishable clothes that might be the common dress of almost any land. The trousers and shirts of the men were mostly white; the women's skirts were of a variety of colors. The people were rather dark complected and reminded Crane of a Mediterranean people who spent much time in the sun. But did these people ever see the sun?

The voice sounded within the ship once more, commanding, "The captain, the admiral, Chief Petty Officer Jones, and Dr. Banks will disembark at once. All other crew members will remain aboard."

Crane and Nelson looked at each other. "I think we have no choice," said Nelson. "But we have an atmosphere problem. We don't know what's outside. It might be something we can breathe, and it might not."

"These people are breathing it."

"Suppose they've been breathing it all their lives—and that it's something we're not used to."

"All their lives! You mean you think they *live* here?"

"It's a city, isn't it? It's not just a base. Maybe it's been here for hundreds of years—perhaps thousands."

Crane wiped perspiration from his face. "You're way ahead of me. But if so, where did they come from?"

"Maybe we're about to find out. At any rate, I think we'd better go out in suits and take our own air with us."

Crane and the three others followed him to the air lock. "They speak English," said Crane finally.

"So they do," said Nelson. "Interesting, isn't it?"

They made their exit through the underwater hatch leading from the air lock, which was actually the only way they could exit into a highly pressurized atmosphere. It had never been anticipated in the design of the *Seaview* that an air lock exit would be necessary in the conning tower.

The four men surfaced near the submarine and found a boat waiting. It contained four guards with weapons that were obviously guns of some type. The seamen were helped in, and the boat moved off, propelled by some silent motive power that was not obvious.

Crane turned on his suit speaker and tried conversation. The strangers around him stared straight ahead.

"I doubt that any of them speak English," said Nelson. "We probably had a special translator speaking to us in the submarine."

"What language do they speak, I wonder?"

Admiral Nelson, seated so that he faced the water, suddenly raised an arm and pointed. His voice was filled with awed disbelief as he spoke. "Look!"

His companions turned. There, beyond the *Seaview*, a giant black hulk was slowly surfacing. Its long, curved back arched up, and its exposed length increased to that of the *Seaview* and beyond—again and again. At last its monstrous bulk was fully evident, dwarfing the *Seaview* like a mother whale and her calf.

"They weren't kidding about the size of that

thing," muttered Curley. "It could swallow us like the whale did Jonah!"

On the dock gestures were made to indicate they should take off their masks and tanks, but Nelson warned his men against it. The strangers gave up and led them along the quay toward the city. The seamen removed the flippers from their feet and walked in the center of the group of guards and the crowd of curious onlookers that gathered.

"I feel like some strange fish that just swam up on the beach," said Curley. "I wonder if they're going to put us in a museum. On the other hand, maybe we'll be lucky if that's all they put us into."

In their diving suits they were partially isolated from the world around them. Crane had a momentary feeling that he was walking in a dream. He turned and looked back to the harbor, where the *Seaview* lay, its passage blocked now by the black hull of the giant, alien submarine. Somehow those aboard that ship knew of the *Seaview* and its crew. They knew his name and that of the Admiral and Dr. Banks and Curley. How, Crane had no idea.

He worried about Cathy. He wished she had not come. If this strange submarine was responsible for the tragedies at Oil City Eighteen and the Corbazzi Mines the outlook was not pleasant.

It was unbearably hot, walking in the suits. The temperature in the cavern was high, both because of its depth and its closeness to the equator. And the open water surface made its humidity extreme.

The public buildings, which they were passing now, were built of white stonework in mixtures of ancient Greek and Roman styles. Homes and small shops were much more simple. They were mostly cubes of irregular size. There were bare openings for windows and doors. There was almost no sign of woodwork. Crane guessed that wood was a very precious commodity here. If they had any, it had to be brought from the surface by submarine.

But obviously they were metalworkers as well

as stone craftsmen. Their great submarine bore that out.

The cavern itself was a mystery. Crane wondered if it were natural or if the people had excavated it. And how had they pressurized it so the sea did not fill it? Or was that a natural condition also? And how was the roof made luminous to provide a great, artificial sky?

Crane wondered if Banks would have any answers, but he didn't question the geologist now. They seemed to be approaching their destination, a magnificent white building with walls and pillars of cut limestone.

They were led up broad steps and into the shadows between the pillars. Something about those pillars struck Crane as odd, yet familiar. He had seen their like somewhere before. They were thicker at the top than at the bottom.

Inside, the men moved through the great entrance hall and along a corridor whose ceiling glowed with phosphorescent light as did the cavern roof.

They came at last to a pair of beautifully

ornamented doors. Bronze, probably, Crane observed, not wood. The doors were opened by two attendants, and the four seamen were ushered forward to enter the room alone. The massive doors closed behind them.

For a moment they thought there was no one else in the broad, high-ceilinged room. Then they were aware of a figure approaching them from their left.

He had been seated at a massive desk that looked as if it were carved from some rare dark wood. The man was of medium height, swarthy, and the abundant hair of his head was graying at the temples. He was dressed in loose white trousers and a blouselike shirt that had no buttons. Leather sandals were on his feet.

He approached the seamen with a smile. "Welcome, gentlemen. Welcome to the city of Minos."

Minos! The word struck Crane's ear like the sound of an echoing bell. He remembered the pillars outside, with tops that were thicker than the bottoms. But it was impossible—

The stranger led the way toward the desk and

indicated chairs. "Please make yourselves comfortable," he said. He took his own chair behind the desk, and then stood up again almost immediately.

"I forgot your hesitation about breathing our air," he said. "It is entirely safe for you, three percent oxygen, ninety-six percent helium, and one percent argon, plus some other inert gases. About the same as you have in your tanks. Also, if you will come with me I will show you suitable garments which can replace those suits and make you much more comfortable."

Nelson cautiously opened his helmet and took a breath of the air in the room. "Seems all right," he said after a moment.

Crane and the others followed his example.

The stranger smiled at them. "Now, let me introduce myself. I am Marpen, the mayor, as you might say—the ruler of the city and the state of Minos. I know who you are, of course. Now, if you wish to exchange the diving suits for more comfortable clothing. . . ."

They followed him into a small adjacent room

where a closet contained clothing suitable for them all. Size and fit were not very important, it appeared, since it seemed customary to wear fairly loose and oversize clothing.

"That is so much better," Marpen announced when they returned to his office. "You will be comfortable now."

"We'd be more comfortable aboard our own ship," said Crane. "Will you tell us why we have been brought here? Who are you people, and what do you want with us?"

"Why have you been brought here?" Marpen exclaimed in mock astonishment. "You haven't been brought. You came voluntarily! You followed my ship for two hundred miles and entered our channels entirely uninvited. It is we who should question *you* as to your intent!"

"You know enough about us to call us by name," said Admiral Nelson. "I suspect the intense magnetic disturbance put out by your ship was partly, at least, a bait to lead us in. We also suspect that such disturbances have a great deal to do with the subsea disasters that have occurred to many of our installations on the seabed."

The smile vanished from the dark face, and Marpen nodded his head in abrupt grimness. "Yes, I know a great deal about you men of the Marine Institute and your proud ship, *Seaview*. I listen to your radio messages, and I have broken your codes. I know where you are and what you are doing. My ships follow you and we see your cities growing and invading our world. And now we are ready to drive you back out of the sea! But first, we want one thing: *Seaview*."

"Who are you?" Nelson demanded. "To what nation do you belong?"

"Who are we?" Marpen smiled softly again. "We are the Sea Kings. And this is our nation!" He swept an arm toward the scene beyond the window. "The sea is our country. We belong to no other!"

"The Sea Kings." Crane felt a cold finger crawling along his spine. "There was a people a long time ago who called themselves the Sea Kings. They had another name, too. Minoans.

And they built great palaces with columns that were thicker at the top than at the bottom."

"We are the Sea Kings," said Marpen simply.

"A *long* time ago," repeated Crane. "Something like thirty-five hundred years. The Sea Kings lived on the isle of Crete."

"They were our fathers," said Marpen. "I see you have been where our people dwelt."

"There was a legend about a great cavern," said Crane slowly, "the Labyrinth."

"Yes. A myth. A fairy tale. And now your scientists congratulate themselves because they think they know the answer to the myth of the Labyrinth. They think it refers to the intricate passageways and corridors of the great palace they have uncovered at Knossos on Crete. How can the fools believe that so great a tale could arise about the halls of a palace? The Labyrinth was real. It led my people to safety when disaster and invasion struck their peaceful isle!"

"Then this is the Labyrinth?"

"No. The Labyrinth was sealed off ages ago. It was utterly destroyed to prevent anyone from the surface from finding us again. But the Labyrinth led us to caverns like these, where we determined to survive against all obstacles and never be driven again.

"We had been the Sea Kings; we would remain kings of the sea. It would be our domain and our life, and no one on the surface would ever drive us again."

"All of which sounds well," said Nelson, "except that it's too much to believe that you found ready-made caverns such as this, complete with helium-oxygen atmosphere and other natural conveniences."

"I didn't say such things were found," snapped Marpen. "Our fathers found dark, cold, miserable caves where they struggled for existence for centuries.

"Slowly, they developed a science. They learned how to generate light and heat for their dark, cold caves. And they burrowed ever deeper and found great openings to undersea worlds. They learned the techniques of undersea living and found natural wells of helium gas to form an atmosphere such as this one. They learned to mine and work metals.

"But our science moved in a different direction than yours. We developed the use of force fields—especially the fields of magnetism and gravity—and learned to put them to such uses and generate them with such power as you have not dreamed of. You have felt the effects of these today in the *Seaview*."

"And so did Oil City Eighteen and the mine village of Corbazzi," said Nelson. "Do you deny that you were responsible for that inhuman destruction?"

"Of course they felt it, just as others will feel it!" said Marpen. "I told you we are the Sea Kings. Centuries ago your people drove mine from the land to the sea. Now the sea is ours. We will drive you from it, just as we were driven long ago."

"There is room enough on this earth for all of us," said Nelson. "On land or in the sea, there is no need for any group to drive others from one place to another."

"Is that what your history of endless wars on the surface proves?"

"We are making progress. There are more people and greater peace than ever before."

"*We* have had no war in all our history in the caves. For thirty-five hundred years the Sea Kings have lived in peace."

"Until now," said Nelson. "Now you attack helpless communities like barbarians of any age."

"The sea is ours," Marpen repeated. "Your attempts to colonize it are invasions."

It was obvious that no amount of reasoning would sway Marpen. But Nelson could not believe that the Sea Kings had known peace for three and one-half millenia under rulers like Marpen. It was more likely that their history had been one of continual strife among themselves, and now they were determined to make suicidal warfare against all the surface nations who were developing the resources of the seas.

"Why have you brought us here?" Crane said again.

"Two reasons. First, while our science is far

ahead of yours in some fields, we have not developed nuclear energy. We want the *Seaview*, and we want the knowledge of the principles on which it operates. Second, now that you have seen what we can do, you are in a position to tell your surface people they must leave the sea to those to whom it belongs."

"You ask the impossible," said Nelson. "We are scientists, but it would take more than this roomful of men to tell you how to make use of nuclear energy. The fuel must be mined and concentrated. We know nothing of that technology. And we cannot tell you how to build a reactor, because we do not know.

"As for warning our people to leave the sea, I am afraid you do not know our people. There is enough in the sea for a hundred times our combined populations. We will cooperate, but we will not be driven out."

"Who can tell how much you are lying?" said Marpen. "But we shall find out as our attacks continue while you remain in confinement here. I am taking the *Theseus*, our submarine, next to one of your surface coastal cities. Consider the effect of what you saw at Oil City or Corbazzi if it were to be repeated at San Francisco or New York!"

6   Prisoners

THE PRISON was more like a luxurious apartment. Each man had his own quarters. There was a central living room, dining room, and a library, all of which they shared.

The library was loaded with volumes from all nations of the surface world, and it held hundreds that were in the Minoan language. Dr. Banks was fascinated by the latter.

"This is almost exactly like the Linear B script found on Crete," he said. "I'm no linguist, but it looks as if it has scarcely changed in all that time. Archaeologists have been trying for years to get a picture of Minoan civilization through a few hundred square inches of clay tablets. What they would give for some of these books!"

Crane regarded their surroundings with wonder. The floor was covered with thick, red carpets. The walls and ceilings were decorated with lavish gold trim and exquisite paintings. Some of the scenes were of the mythical gods and goddesses of ancient Crete. Some were of surface scenes. Others were vivid scenes of the undersea world, with a brilliance that the seamen had never seen.

Ornate chandeliers provided electric light. The rooms seemed warmed by some kind of radiant heating system at night, when a strange, cool wind seemed to blow through the cavern.

"Imagine the civilization and technology behind all this," said Crane. "Somewhere in these caverns are the factories, the rug mills, the electric plants that supply all this. We need to cooperate and trade with these people, not make war with them."

"Seems to me," said Curley, "that it'll be something of a job to convince this Marpen fellow of that."

"You can hardly blame them, in one respect,"

said Banks. "Look at it from their point of view. It's something like the take-over of America from the Indians. There were resources enough for Indians and white men alike—but who got them?"

"I think we've learned something since the days of the Indian wars," said Nelson. "No one knew until now that the Minoans existed. They attacked our settlements without even giving a clue to their existence. Now that we know, I think the civilized nations are capable of sharing in the sea without oppressing the Minoans."

"Well, as Curley says," Crane muttered, "it's going to be awfully hard to convince Marpen of that. And, in the meantime, just what are we going to do about our present predicament? If Marpen's weapon—whatever it is—is as powerful against a surface city as it was at Oil City Eighteen and Corbazzi, he could wipe it out. There's no debate about the rightness or wrongness of that. We've got to stop it somehow!"

"If we could get to the *Seaview*," said Nelson, "we could detonate a nuclear torpedo in the harbor and wipe out their submarine and their city —as well as ourselves. But that would only postpone the disaster. The world would still not know of the Minoans, and they would be free to regroup and attack later. We've got to get word to the outside, as well as destroy them."

"Which means getting back to the *Seaview*," said Crane. "We've got to make a break for it, somehow."

"Those guards aren't all over the place for nothing," said Curley. "And, besides, I've been looking around. This place is wired like a telephone exchange. You can bet your solid gold inlays that they're listening to every word we're saying. Not only that, they're watching every move we make. For instance, that squid in the painting on the wall over there has a TV camera in its eye. I'd cover it up, but there are at least a dozen more, including one in the ceiling.

"The rooms are crisscrossed by infrared beams to keep tab on our movements in the dark. Whatever we do has got to be done by brainpower, not muscle!"

Crane moved to the window, which looked out from the tower in which they were held. He could see the harbor and the two submarines. In the two days they had been held, there had been considerable activity around the *Theseus.* Guards were posted on the *Seaview,* and the hatches had been opened to the pressurized atmosphere. He thought of Cathy and Sea Baby and all the crew. He wondered if any message had been given them regarding those who were being held.

Then, as he watched, a faint movement occurred in the harbor. It was a familiar movement to a submarine man, and Crane cried out to his companions. "They're leaving. Marpen's leaving!"

They rushed to the window. The *Theseus* was slowly submerging. The long, black arch of the submarine's back shortened. Then it was gone, and only the conning tower remained. It moved away from the city as the ship gathered speed. Then it, too, disappeared, and the *Seaview* remained alone in the harbor.

Which city would it be? Was the *Theseus* heading for New York or San Francisco, as Marpen had threatened? Or would it be another —Miami, New Orleans—

They did not know how the *Theseus* was powered, but Marpen had said they lacked nuclear energy. That probably meant that with as much as twenty-four hours' lead the *Theseus* could still be overtaken by the *Seaview* before the Minoans could attack. The instruments of the *Seaview* were still locked on the Minoan submarine, unless they had been discovered and turned off by Marpen's men. So the crewmen had twenty-four hours at a maximum to find some means of escape and get the *Seaview* on its way.

Crane stared at the admiral without speaking, and each knew the other was thinking the same desperate thought: How could they escape to the *Seaview* in time to overtake Marpen?

The light of the cavern sky dimmed in simulation of a surface twilight. Guards brought their evening meal of exquisite food. Each time the guards entered, the seamen found it difficult to restrain themselves from jumping them. But they knew it would be folly. The guards were heavily armed, and the building was certainly full of them.

It had to be, as Curley had said, by brainpower, not muscle.

"Let's enjoy the food while it's here," said Curley. "Who knows when they might decide to stop feeding us?"

"You're right," said Crane. "And maybe it'll nourish that needed brainpower, too."

Curley looked at him and winked. "Right you are, Captain."

The sky light dimmed to darkness. There were TV and radio pickups from the surface available to them, and the Minoans had broadcast entertainment in their own language and customs. Crane, Nelson, and Curley were too weighed down by the futility of their position to desire any of this. But Banks spent hours watching and listening to the Minoan entertainment. Every aspect of the culture of the Sea Kings was so thrilling to him as a scientist that the others wondered at times if he had forgotten they were prisoners.

Curley finally became so irritated by the sound of the Minoan programs that he could stand it no longer. "Can't you please turn that junk off for tonight, Dr. Banks? It's driving us out of our minds, and we've got more important things to think about!"

Banks smiled at his companions and turned the instrument off. He got up and joined the others. "Don't think my enjoyment of our hosts' entertainment is entirely fruitless," he said.

"They aren't hosts, remember," said Curley. "They're jailers."

"At any rate," Banks continued, "their entertainment tells a good deal about themselves, which we might find useful."

"What do you mean?" asked Nelson. "Remember, they're listening."

"It doesn't matter. But consider this: Suppose a complete stranger, one who did not understand our language, should see and hear our own television programs. What would these programs tell him about us as a people?"

"Not very much," said Curley. "Look at the mistaken ideas that people of different countries have about each other as a result of seeing only plays and motion pictures."

"But those are the opinions of the common people. I'm talking about a visitor who is a capable scientist."

"Who knows what an egghead could make of our TV?"

"What are you getting at?" said Nelson.

"I'm no expert psychologist," said Banks, "but I think I've had enough scientific training to interpret a few things displayed in the entertainment of these people. Two of them are important to us.

"First, I'm sure I detect frequent references to the surface and to our people. So the common citizen here knows of the surface peoples. And the attitude, as far as I can make out, is without hostility. There is no indication of a desire to make war on the surface peoples."

"That could mean that the hostility exists only

at the top, among a small group," said Crane.

"It's entirely possible," said Banks. "The second factor I detect is a strong reverence for royalty. Their government is evidently a monarchy, and it has every evidence of great popular support."

"That could be just propaganda," said Curley.

"Possibly. But I don't think so. It's not difficult to distinguish propaganda from genuine enthusiasm when you're on the outside."

"But how can you be so certain of these things when you can't even understand the language?" said Nelson.

"I'm not certain. But in the actions I detect enough of what I consider substantial evidence to show these things are so."

"So Marpen can count on the strong backing of the people for anything he does, just because he's royalty. Is that it?" asked Crane.

"Yes—*if* Marpen were royalty."

"What do you mean? Isn't he?" asked Nelson.

"I don't think so. He's certainly not the king, nor even a prince. He's some kind of governing official. Mayor, he called himself."

"Then where's the king? Why haven't we seen or heard of him?"

"I think we've got a situation here where there is a strong division of the people. Marpen represents a rebellious minority opposing the king—whoever *he* is. I doubt very much that there is either popular support or royal support among this people for an attack on the surface."

"A lot of good it does to know that," said Curley, "with Marpen and his pirates on the way to wipe out some coast city the way he did Oil City and Corbazzi—and Anatolia Copper."

"It might do us a lot of good," said Banks. He drew a pencil and an old envelope from his inside coat pocket and scrawled idly on it for a moment. Then he got up and went to the instrument. "Well, if you don't mind, I'd like to watch just a little more before bedtime. It really won't disturb you too much, will it, Curley?"

"Aw, I guess not. Go ahead, Doc, and don't mind me. I'll go to bed when I get tired."

Nelson picked up a Minoan book and idly

scanned the pictures. But out of the corner of his eye he glanced at the envelope Banks had left on the arm of the chair. It read:

> If I am right, it would do us a great deal of good to contact the loyal followers of the king. And I think we should be prepared to take advantage of a possible attempt by *them* to contact *us!*

Before they went to bed that night Nelson managed to slip the note to Crane and to Curley. Each of them glanced at it and read it without expression.

Unable to share their thoughts because of the constantly spying eyes and ears, they retired with their minds in a turmoil. Crane stood for a long time by the window of his room. It overlooked a portion of the city, and from the corner of it he could see the shadowy outline of the *Seaview* in the harbor. He longed for some way to get a message to Cathy and to learn if she was all right. There had to be a way out! Why couldn't they think of something?

He turned back to the bed and lay down. He

tossed and rolled for what seemed like hours before he dropped into uneasy sleep. When he did, his head was filled with nightmares. He dreamed he was alone in the midst of the sea, swimming at great depths. Frantically he pursued a great, black submarine that carried the death of the world in its hull. Behind him hordes of deadly sharks and killer whales pursued relentlessly. He woke from time to time, bathed in sweat, and then dropped into fitful sleep again.

At last he dreamed his way into calm, green seas, and the sun was shining pleasantly. He was on the warm shore and someone was near, whispering softly, "I am your friend. Come with me. I am your friend."

The soft voice soothed the turmoil within him. It sounded almost like the voice of Cathy. But that couldn't be. She was on the *Seaview*, and the *Seaview* was—

He bolted upright in bed. In the dim shadows of the room he could make out the dark outline of a figure beside the bed, kneeling on the floor. With an instinctive gesture of defense he lunged out to grasp the stranger by the wrist and throat, twisting to keep a possible knife from plunging at him. The figure went down to the floor, crying faintly in protest.

Crane jerked away in shock and surprise. It was a woman.

She struggled to a sitting position on the floor while Crane leaned closer. "You—you were whispering. It was *you* I heard in my sleep! Who are you?" he demanded.

"Do not talk," the woman whispered faintly. "They will hear us. I come to help you. Get the others and follow me. Do exactly as I do. Do not speak louder than this. Will you come?"

For a moment Crane wondered if this were some kind of weird trap set by the Minoans. Then he thought of Banks's prediction of the previous evening: "We should be prepared to take advantage of a possible attempt by them to contact us!"

This could be it! Crane was going to gamble that Banks had guessed right. He knew the others would agree.

"I'll come," he whispered.

Immediately the woman began crawling along the floor toward the doorway. She was not on hands and knees, but pressed as close to the floor as possible. Crane had a fleeting impression of a soldier crawling through an attack of gunfire.

Then he realized she was doing it to avoid breaking the infrared detector beams that crisscrossed all the rooms, and thereby betraying their movement to some distant spy center.

Hugging close to the floor, he slipped into the Minoan shirt and trousers and sandals, then began to wriggle his way slowly toward Nelson's room.

He knew the admiral well enough to duck as Nelson woke up and swung at the object of his disturbance. "It's me," Crane whispered. "Calm down and listen. There's a woman in the living room who wants us to follow her. It's either the thing Banks predicted, or somebody's out there with a chopper waiting for us. I'm for gambling it's what Banks said."

Nelson's response was instantaneous. "Right. Let's go."

He slipped into his clothes. They agreed Nelson would get Banks, and Crane would get Curley. Ten minutes later they assembled in the living room. Crane moved up beside their unknown guide and whispered, "We're ready."

Without answering, she began the slow, crablike movement that carried her toward the door. Crane saw now that it was open, and the hall beyond was utterly dark. The group made their way through the doorway until the cold stone floor of the hall was beneath them. Here the woman stood up. The four men arose to their feet.

The woman took Crane's arm and whispered, "Come."

As he turned to follow, Crane glimpsed in the shadows the forms of the two guards who had stood by the doorway. A dark pool, which might have been blood, stained the white stonework beside each of them.

They moved quickly along the short length

of hall. Then two additional strangers appeared from around a corner. The seamen tensed for attack, but their guide whispered quickly, "They are with me!"

Silently the group moved to the stairway and down long flights in total darkness, touching the walls for guidance. Crane tried to estimate the distance by the number of steps. He was certain at last that they must be well underground. But the steps continued. They were broken by short passageways, and several times the seamen heard the opening of doors and felt their way past the portals.

Then down again—

There was a long passage with rough walls and an uneven floor, which seemed to be some kind of natural cavern. And then a ponderous door slid aside and they heard the lap of water.

There was a small light beyond. A narrow rock ledge jutted into the black waters of an underground channel. Two small boats were tied up. A guard watched with tense alertness.

The three Minoan men and the woman exchanged words in their own language, then directed the seamen to divide up, two to a boat. Two Minoans got into each boat.

Crane looked along the black waterway into the murky darkness. He thought of a secret moat under some ancient castle and wondered for a moment if this were still part of the nightmare he'd been having an hour ago. Santa Barbara, the Institute, the *Seaview,* Cathy—where were they?

With Nelson he climbed into the lead boat and accepted one of the oars offered by the Minoan. The Minoan guard was in front, the woman guide behind. The other four were similarly seated in the rear boat.

The boatman attached his tiny light to the bow and pushed away from the ledge. The water was almost still, except for a small current flowing toward them. They headed the boats into it, paddling quietly.

7

The Sea King

A SPECK OF light drifting in a darkened artery. An eternity of silence, except for the dip and splash of the oars. No one spoke, except when the woman guide once addressed a quiet remark to her companions in the musical Minoan tongue. No answer was given.

Crane's arms began to tire from the awkward and unaccustomed paddling. But there was still no end to the darkness and the silence and the black water. It seemed as if this toilsome journey were destined to continue forever.

Even as he wondered, the lead oarsman gave a sharp sideward push with his oar and guided the boat into a dark recess in the cavern wall. It was deep, and they paddled for another two or three hundred feet before they came within range of a tiny light glowing on a rocky pier.

When they reached it, the Minoans docked and quickly tied the boats. They were joined by another, who held the light at the dock, as if waiting for them.

They led the seamen up a sloping path that was slippery with moisture. After a quarter of a mile, as Crane estimated it, they finally emerged from the mouth of the tunnel. The sky of the cavern was beginning to brighten in a faint, artificial dawn.

Crane and his companions looked about and saw that they were in some remote region at a distance from the city, which could be seen a mile or two behind them. An arm of the harbor extended below them. The terrain of the cavern was rough, with miniature rolling hills. Except for the cavern roof above, it might have been a scene on some Grecian coast.

"Come." The woman guide spoke hastily and beckoned them on. For the first time they got a good look at her and saw that she was a young

woman, perhaps in her late twenties. Her hair
was black and long about her shoulders, bound
with a bright metal clip. She wore a blue skirt
and blouse of material that had the fineness and
rustle of silk.

They followed her to the top of a low rise
and saw in a small hollow a rambling, one-story
house of stone. In spite of its isolation there was
an unmistakable touch of luxury about it.

There was grassy growth on the hill, as high
as their ankles. In the pale morning light its
color seemed a lighter, more delicate green than
any they had seen before, and the shape of the
blades was not like that of any grass of the surface world. Crane wondered how it or any living
thing could survive in the total absence of sunlight. But there it was. The light of the cavern
must have some of the characteristics of sunlight.

They crossed an open plaza before the house.
Armed guards were stationed casually at a score
of unobtrusive posts. Obviously they had been
there throughout the night.

The main hall of the house was brilliantly

lit, but to the seamen it looked empty at first glance. The Minoans, however, proceeded directly to the far end at the left with stately steps. They halted with a reverent bow.

Behind a massive table of carved stone a small, thin man of untold age sat as if waiting through an endless time. He did not move as the Minoans saluted him and remained immobile, bowed from the waist. Then a change of expression on the old face released them. They straightened and parted on either side, and the four seamen found themselves facing the ancient Minoan alone.

"This is the one!" Banks whispered hoarsely. *"This* is the king!"

A trace of a smile broke the austerity of the old man's face. "There must be something of royalty left in these withered lines, after all," he said, "if even a stranger can recognize the King of the Sea."

"We salute your highness," said Banks. He gave a short bow of courtesy. His companions joined in it.

"Thank you, men of the *Seaview*. And welcome to the land of Minos. Your reception so far has been a poor one, but the circumstances have not been entirely within our control. I know your names, but I cannot match faces with them. Will you introduce yourselves, please?"

Admiral Nelson introduced himself and his companions.

"Thank you," said the Minoan. "As for me, I am known as Pharon, King of the Sea. As you have seen, my kingship is not always acknowledged, but I am, nevertheless, King of the Minoans.

"Now—let chairs be brought and let us sit around the table. There is much to discuss. Breakfast will be served while we meet."

"If you please, Your Highness," said Nelson urgently, "it seems obvious that Marpen is an enemy of yours as well as ours. You have rescued us from him, perhaps for purposes of your own, but Marpen is on his way to destroy our cities. Our only hope of preventing that is to follow him and destroy him. But time is urgent. Every minute of delay lessens our chance of overtaking him."

"I know Marpen's plans," said Pharon. "I freed you so that you might pursue him. But there are two things you do not know. One is that you have no chance of boarding the *Seaview* unless I am with you. Second, you would have no chance of survival in a pitched battle with the *Theseus* without certain defenses which I must supply. You have already tasted the might of the *Theseus*. What power do you have to stand against that?"

"The time—"

"I am aware of the problem, Admiral. The goal of the *Theseus* is your city of Miami, and time is indeed short. But without the defenses I must provide, your mission is as futile as if you were too late."

"We have torpedoes with nuclear warheads!"

"Which could never approach the *Theseus* because they would be destroyed first."

Reluctantly Nelson and his companions joined

the Minoans about the table. Dishes and heaping platters of food were brought in.

"What are the defenses you speak of?" asked Nelson.

"You experienced only a faint touch of the power of the weapons of the *Theseus,*" said Pharon. "The full power of them would have shaken the *Seaview* to pieces and sent the fragments to the bottom of the harbor. The same power can destroy your torpedoes before they ever reach their goal.

"The defense I speak of is one which can be installed in the *Seaview* to counteract and absorb the force of the intense vibrations generated by Marpen's weapons. Units can also be installed in your torpedoes to protect them until they reach their target. We have prepared these defenses and will help you install them in your ship."

"When?"

"Work has been continuing in our royal laboratories since you arrived. It is nearly finished. Within an hour you shall be on your way. In the meantime, I can only offer my futile regrets for the actions of Marpen and pray that you may be successful against him."

"You do not oppose our colonization and use of the sea?" asked Crane.

"There is more sea than earth. And it is far richer. There is enough for all. Except for Marpen, you would never have learned of us."

"You know a great deal about us," said Nelson. "How do so many of you know our language? Through our broadcasts?"

"We've lived among you and gone to school with you," said Pharon. "Why should we not understand you?"

"What?" exclaimed Crane. "You mean some of you have actually come to the surface and gone to our schools?"

"Why not? We establish citizenship in many countries. We mingle and we learn. But always we come home to the sea. I am a British subject, officially. Marpen but lately graduated in California. Would that he might have learned some of the things taught in my day!"

"Then there's not much you don't know about

us," said Crane. "But Marpen said he wanted the *Seaview* for its nuclear secrets."

"Yes. We have duplicated many of your sciences and have discovered much that your own scientists have never approached. But nuclear science is one that has eluded us. So much is not taught in your schools, but is held as military secrets—which is as it must be with those like Marpen in the world.

"The monstrous size of the *Theseus* is caused by the need for cruder types of power for her great weapons. And because of her size she needs greater power to run through the sea."

"How many like the *Theseus* do you have?" asked Crane.

"Only one. When you have destroyed the *Theseus* you will be safe."

"You will build more."

"Not if Marpen is destroyed along with the submarine."

"He has followers."

"He has some foolish men who will realize their foolishness when he is gone. But he has no followers. I am the king. They follow me."

"I don't understand," said Nelson.

"No, you wouldn't. An Englishman might, but not an American."

"What do you mean by that?"

"Among us, the king is regarded so deeply that it takes Marpen's special kind of insanity to oppose him. But even those who have allowed themselves to be swayed by this insanity do not oppose the king."

"With your pardon—it looks as if there's considerable opposition."

"Am I in chains or in prison?" Pharon held up his thin arms. "I come and I go. Marpen occupies certain offices of the government, but I move freely because I am king even to those who are persuaded to Marpen."

"You are saying they have assumed some of your powers, but they dare not hurt your person or your liberty."

"Yes. In a way, that is correct. I am the King of the Sea."

There was a sudden cry from the end of the

table where sat the woman who had guided the seamen to freedom. She was on her feet, shaking her fist. "You know what you say is not true! They have killed the King of the Sea!"

Pharon glanced at her sympathetically. "I was the Sea King long ago," he said to the seamen. "Afterward my son ruled, and he died. Then my grandson ruled, and Nessia is his Queen. My grandson was killed in a sea hunt. Accidentally, it was said. But we know that Marpen killed him. Marpen is not afraid to kill. He does not revere the throne of the Sea Kings. He seeks it for himself.

"After my grandson was gone there was no one left. I took the throne once again in my old age. But I saw that Marpen would soon conquer. There was no one left, that is, except the infant son of Nessia. And Marpen would not stop at the murder of a child. I had to see that he was put beyond the reach of Marpen.

"That is why I gave him to you."

"Sea Baby!" exclaimed Crane. "The prince of Minos—you left him in the ruins of Oil City?"

Pharon nodded. "Sooner or later, even if it was only upon my death, Marpen would gain control, and he would destroy the prince. So we took one of our small ships while Marpen was away. The plan was Nessia's. We left the Prince in the oilman's hut an hour before you arrived. He was quite safe, of course. We prepared the stage to make you believe he was a survivor of Oil City, and we stood by a short distance from you to make sure you discovered and removed him safely. We thank you for your care, and trust he is well at your headquarters."

"He is well," said Crane, "but he is not at headquarters. He is aboard the *Seaview*. We dared not decompress him fast enough to get him out before we left to search for the *Theseus*."

Nessia gave a small cry. A flood of Minoan words burst from her lips. Then she turned to the seamen. "My baby. You can let me see my baby once more!"

Pharon raised his hand gently for silence and attention. "This news is both surprising and shocking. We sent the prince to you for his own protection. It was the only place Marpen could not reach him. We felt he was safe; now he is in the midst of dangers again."

"With Marpen continuing his attacks on our sea cities, it was urgent that we pursue him," said Nelson. "And it was for the baby's best interest that he be decompressed slowly aboard the submarine. We didn't even know that he could be safely decompressed."

"Of course," said Pharon, "and again, let me say we are grateful. I offer no criticism for anything that has happened. In fact, all that has happened has been our responsibility, not yours."

"What do you mean?" asked Crane.

"We expected things to happen as they have. We planned to take advantage of them. We knew you would pursue Marpen and track him here."

"How could you know that?"

"It was inevitable. You were certain to recognize that the disasters to your sea cities were not natural. And we knew you would then follow the cause of the disaster to its source.

"Marpen has long been our enemy. But he

has now made himself your enemy as well. And we planned that when he did, we would provide you the protection that would enable you to defeat the *Theseus* in pitched battle.

"We planned long as to how we would remove you from Marpen's imprisonment. Many of our followers are in his organization. Construction of the protective devices for the *Seaview* was started long ago.

"What we didn't plan was that the prince should share the peril of the decisive battle with the *Theseus*. But perhaps it is just as well. He is the Prince of the Sea Kings. If we are successful in defeating Marpen, it is a fitting inauguration of his kingship. If we are defeated, it is as well that he should perish with us."

"He needn't be aboard at all," said Crane. "We can take him out of decompression now, and leave him with your people."

Pharon shook his head. "As long as Marpen is alive, the prince is not safe here."

"I don't believe you should be aboard, either, during our pursuit of the *Theseus*," said Nelson.

"Then there will be no battle with the *Theseus*. You will never live to board the *Seaview* again."

"I don't understand." Nelson's face flushed with sudden anger. "Surely you don't mean to threaten us."

Pharon laughed bitterly. "No, my friends. The only threat to you among the Minoans is from Marpen. But there is only one way you can even approach your ship."

"How?"

"With me going before you."

Nessia burst out, "You mustn't let him do it! He thinks he must lead you personally through the streets of the city where all the people can see him. He thinks they won't harm him because he is king. But Marpen's followers will kill him. He'll never get near the ship. Nor will you. You mustn't let him go. There are other ways!"

"I'm afraid we don't follow all of this," said Nelson. "Why must you go with us, Your Highness? And what other ways are there, Nessia?"

The queen began to speak again, but Pharon silenced her with a raised hand. "There is danger, and Nessia would spare me from it."

"It's utterly hopeless!" cried Nessia.

"The ship is under guard," said Pharon, "and every possible approach is cut off. Even if you had your diving gear—which you haven't—you could not approach through the water. Automatic detectors would discover you, and Marpen's men would kill you.

"The only possible approach is a direct one. I will lead you through the city, and no one will harm you. Aboard the *Seaview* I will dismiss Marpen's guards, and you will be free to sail. And I shall remain with you. I shall see with my own eyes the destruction of Marpen. If he is not destroyed, I have no wish to return."

"If the rebels are in the streets you will be in danger," said Nelson. "How can it be otherwise?"

"I am the king. You see, for centuries the royal family has been father and mother to the Minoans. We have given them justice and law and progression up from the foul caves they first inhabited when they came down from the surface. And they have given us loyalty and love.

"There have been enemies, of course. And never so many as now. But they are yet in a minority. They tell the people the king is old, and he can no longer lead them. They say these are new times, which the king cannot comprehend. There are many who believe these things. Yet they revere the king, as they would an old father who must be cared for because he can no longer stand as a father to his sons.

"Marpen knows that the quickest way to assure failure for himself would be to allow harm to come to me. Though they turn away, I am never so safe as when I am among my people."

"Then why is the prince not safe?" asked Nelson.

"The prince is not the king. And there are so many ways an infant can be destroyed without apparent blame or cause. Marpen knows exactly how far he can go, and how far he must not go. His followers know it, too. I am safe among them."

"You must not believe him!" cried Nessia. "He is an old man who lets past loyalties delude him.

The people now do not know he exists. They do not harm him because he does not matter. But if he tries to lead you to the *Seaview* you will all be killed!"

Pharon smiled indulgently upon his daughter-in-law again. Just then a messenger approached and bent to give the king his message.

Pharon nodded and the messenger went away. "It is not easy to be an old man," Pharon said slowly, "much less an old king. Your friends think you don't know what you're talking about, and try to do things for your own good. Worst of all, sometimes they're right.

"But I assure you there is no other way in this matter. Only in this way can you take the neutralizer equipment with you, for one thing. And without it, you are dead men. Finally, you simply have no choice. You agree to my plan or the neutralizers will not be supplied you. And I have just received word that they are ready. I think there is no time to lose!"

8   Escape

THE MINOANS had cars for surface trans-
portation within the limits of their underground domain. The cars were magnetically
powered. They were completely open, since there
was neither sun nor rain, and they traveled at
modest speeds that didn't require protection from
the wind. Otherwise, they were luxurious even
by the automobile standards of the surface
world.

Ten of the cars had been drawn up in line outside Pharon's suburban residence. In addition to
the drivers, they held members of Pharon's staff
who would form the necessary retinue for an
informal procession to the harbor. Provision was
made for the seamen, and one of the cars held

the neutralizer equipment, carefully shrouded and guarded.

The four seamen entered the car assigned to them, but they felt highly uncertain about the whole procedure. It was hard to evaluate Pharon. Was he a wise and courageous old ruler? Or was he a forgotten and deluded old man, as Nessia had said?

Curley was violently opposed. "Maybe they won't shoot the king," he said, "but what's to prevent Marpen's bandits from knocking us off one by one? Maybe Pharon doesn't have to worry about his hide, but I'm plenty worried about mine!"

"You have company in your worry," said Crane, "but we're pretty well boxed in. The king is gambling on some intangible regard for the royal family, which may or may not exist. And he's backing that belief with his own life. With our lives we're backing a gamble on a chance to save millions of lives in our coastal cities. It's as Pharon said, we simply have no choice."

The procession moved slowly from the house

along the uneven road leading to the city. The seamen were directly behind the car of King Pharon and Queen Nessia. Three cars of royal retainers rode in front. Trumpeters and flag bearers were in the lead.

Crane was heartened as they neared the edge of the city and passed the first of the scattered private homes. In each there was a sudden flurry of activity as the royal procession was recognized. Those inside the houses and in the tiny fields nearby were called and came running. At the edge of the road they stopped respectfully—even reverently, Nelson thought.

Pharon smiled at his people and raised his hand in greeting. Nessia did likewise, but she seemed frozen by her fear. The royal attendants also seemed uncertain. Of all those in the procession, Pharon alone was completely at ease and confident of his people.

The crowds increased as they neared the city. Crane and his companions began to relax at the evidence of fulfillment of Pharon's trust in his people. The Minoans dropped whatever they were doing and lined the streets in genuine enthusiasm.

The procession came to the heart of the city. Some of the buildings were four or five stories high here. In the windows above, Crane could see faces that were not smiling, hands that were not waving. They were few, but these people remained stolid and unmoved as their king passed by. It was among these, Crane thought, that Marpen had his recruits. And any one of them might be hiding a weapon that would be drawn the moment the procession was past.

Crane glanced ahead. Pharon had seen these stolid ones, too. He waved deliberately in their direction. They did not return his greeting. The muscles of Pharon's neck throbbed with sudden tension. His skin paled.

Then Crane knew that the old man was not deceived. Pharon understood better than any of them the risk he was taking. It was his risk, not Nessia's, not that of the men of the *Seaview*.

Only one thing stood between Pharon and death: the rebels' knowledge that any harm to the king would turn the Minoan citizens against the rebels. Pharon's safety and that of all his companions depended on how thoroughly Marpen had drilled this fact into the minds of his rebels.

Pharon was a brave man, Crane thought—one of the bravest he had ever known. The king waved and smiled to the crowd, knowing each moment could be his last if he had miscalculated.

The crowd saw that the procession was headed for the harbor. At the quay the throngs increased until they almost blocked the street. But the cars stopped at last at the dock where the royal boat had been drawn up. Preceded by their retainers, Pharon and Nessia stepped out. Hastily gathered flowers were thrown in their path as they walked toward the dock.

The four seamen began to breathe easier. It looked as if they had made it. But there was one big hurdle still ahead—the guards aboard the *Seaview*.

The boat was large enough for the entire group, plus the neutralizer equipment, which was carefully loaded aboard. The distance to the *Seaview* was covered quickly. As the group approached, the Minoan guards on the deck of the submarine came to attention. One of them called out in a challenging tone that seemed to Crane to hold contempt and derision, although he could not understand the Minoan words.

Those in the boat made no answer. Instead Pharon rose with royal dignity and stood with feet spread apart and arms folded as the boat nudged the hull of the *Seaview*. Crane and Curley caught the recessed handholds and mooring rings and made the boat fast. Pharon stepped to the deck of the submarine.

Immediately the guard near the open door of the conning tower stepped forward and barred the king's way.

"We've got trouble!" said Nelson. "Get up there, fast!"

He and Crane climbed to the deck, followed by Curley and Banks. They paired off on each side of Pharon. The other guards on the deck tensed but made no move to advance.

The guard blocking Pharon's way spoke

sharply again, and Pharon answered quietly in Minoan. Nessia later told them what was said.

"Who comes aboard the Devil's ship?" the guard asked.

"The Sea King comes," Pharon answered. "Make the path clear for your king."

"This is not the territory of the Sea King."

"The Sea King goes where he wills. Make the path clear!"

The tension was obvious to the seamen even though they did not understand the words.

"We've got to take him," said Nelson. "I'll draw his attention. You jump him from that side."

Crane nodded. This guard was the dangerous one. The others would not rush, at least not until it was too late.

Nelson yelled, "Get out of the way!"

The guard didn't understand the words, but he understood the menace. He turned and took a step toward Nelson. Crane leaped and pinned the man's arms behind his back. Nelson grasped his legs. Together they swept him up and heaved him into the water.

Crane whirled back to the two guards on his side of the deck. Curley joined him, while Nelson and Banks faced the other two.

"Wait!" Pharon called.

The seamen halted but kept their eyes on the four guards. Pharon spoke briefly and commandingly. The guards glanced uncertainly at their companion, who was now swimming frantically for shore. Then they dropped their arms.

"There must be more inside the submarine," said Crane.

"Eight more, they said," said Pharon. "I'm sure we can—"

He was interrupted by a cry from Nessia. "Look!" She pointed toward the shore. A half dozen boats were setting out. One was headed for the swimming guard.

"They are Marpen's," Pharon said. "There isn't time to rout the guards inside and eject them. We'll have to take them along and get under way at once."

The neutralizers were being lifted carefully to the deck of the *Seaview*. Crane peered into the conning tower and down the open hatch. No one was in sight. He nodded to Pharon.

Crane wondered about his own crew. It was hard to imagine that his men wouldn't have found some way to overcome so few guards.

There was a complication in allowing Pharon to go first into the ship. If one of the seamen should encounter him he would surely attack the king, not knowing the situation. Crane hurried after Pharon, to be sure of reaching the deck as soon as the king.

The only occupant of the watch deck to which they descended was a Minoan guard. His face paled as he recognized Pharon. The king uttered a single word, and the man lowered his gun and bowed his head. Pharon told him he was to be a member of the king's retinue for the duration of the voyage. The guard thanked him profusely and answered all the questions Pharon put to him.

"He says three guards are stationed in the control room," Pharon told Crane. "They are armed and threaten to destroy the ship's controls if any attempt is made to interfere with them.

That is how they kept the crew subdued."

Crane hated to think of the results if a guard went berserk and turned a gun on the controls of the *Seaview*.

Behind them they heard the sound of loading the neutralizers and the closing of the conning tower door and hatches. Pharon's party must be all aboard in the cramped conning tower.

"Let's go this way, then," said Crane.

A dull clamoring on the outside of the hull told them the party which had set out from the docks had arrived and was beating the hull in the wrath of their frustration.

Crane and Pharon reached the open entrance of the control room. No one could be seen inside. "Stay out of sight," said Pharon, "until you know I have succeeded or failed."

Every instinct told Crane not to allow Pharon to enter the control room. But they had trusted the aged king so far, and everything had occurred just as he had predicted.

Crane waited. A full minute passed. Then there was an exclamation in Minoan and a short burst of Minoan conversation. It was broken by the sudden whine of a Minoan gun and a scream of agony. Crane seized the weapon he had taken from the guard by the conning tower and ran into the control room.

He expected to see Pharon lying on the floor. But it wasn't Pharon. It was one of the guards. The Sea King was just inside the doorway, facing the guards beyond. He was pointing a small hand weapon toward his enemies.

Crane moved up slowly. "I didn't know you were armed."

Pharon smiled grimly. "Do you think I would be fool enough to come into a situation like this without arms? That one"—he gestured toward the unmoving guard on the floor—" was once one of my palace guards. Marpen won him over in the very beginning. He had nothing to lose. I had to use the only kind of reasoning he understood. These other two—they will give us no trouble."

Crane exhaled with relief and stepped to the microphone by the command station. He switched it to all compartments.

"This is your captain," he said. "Repeat: This is the captain. Stay where you are and listen carefully. We are again in command of the ship and will get under way in a few minutes. The king of the Minoans and his staff are aboard. He will now speak to the Minoan guards, commanding them to lay down their arms and proceed to the main wardroom. If they obey the king's command I want the senior officer who observes such action to report to me at once. Your silence will indicate they have refused to obey, in which case we will go through the ship and hunt them down."

Pharon stepped to the microphone and spoke slowly and with authority. He finished, and they waited. The minutes passed. Three, four, five—

Then Mason, the executive officer, spoke over the intercom. "They finally did it," he said. "It looked for a moment as if they were going to try to blow up the place rather than surrender, but we have their guns, and they're on the way to the wardroom. What are your orders, Captain?"

Crane felt an urge to sit down, as if he were suddenly deflated. The massive tension of his body released abruptly and left him limp. He looked at the others, who had come up behind Pharon. He could sense they shared his relief. Nelson was smiling.

"My orders are to get under way immediately in pursuit of the *Theseus*," said Crane. "Does this have your approval, Admiral?"

"My deepest approval," said Nelson. "Full speed!"

"All Watch Number Two crewmen assume duties," said Crane. "Report when ready."

One by one the various compartments and stations reported ready. The reactor room. The diving stand. The navigator. The helmsmen. The planesmen. The chief petty officer of the watch in charge of the ballast control panel—

Crane turned the command over to Mason. "Make way out of this channel and pursue the *Theseus* at maximum speed."

He noted the clock on the wall. It was just twenty hours since the *Theseus* had departed.

Because the hatches had been opened in the harbor the entire ship was now pressurized for nine hundred feet water depth. That meant that Sea Baby and Cathy in the decompression chamber were at a lower pressure than the rest of them. Crane could see no reason to continue the decompression of the prince. He would be going back to Minos—or none of them would.

He took Pharon and Nessia with him to the lower deck and the decompression chamber. Cathy had her face pressed against the port of the chamber. She had heard all of the conversation on the intercom. As Crane came up she couldn't keep the tears out of her eyes, but she scolded over the intercom, "You must have taken time to polish every rail and dust every corner of the ship before coming down to see me."

Crane grinned and ignored her scolding. "I do the important things first. One of these is that I have found Sea Baby's mother, and this is his great-grandfather. We've got a long story to tell you. But first you can get out of the decompression chamber. Sea Baby will be going home, and he lives at nine hundred feet sea depth."

Cathy stared uncomprehendingly. For the time

being she was without words. Crane opened the valves to equalize the pressure slowly between the interior of the submarine and the decompression chamber.

Nessia was crying as the door of the chamber opened at last. Without waiting for Cathy to bring the baby out, she burst in and grasped him in her arms. In Minoan she crooned softly to him and hugged him to her breast. Crane led Cathy outside.

Once outside, he introduced Cathy to Pharon and to Nessia. "We've got a long story to tell," he repeated. "Let's make ourselves comfortable while we tell it."

They went back to the upper deck and sat by the great bow ports of the observation room while Crane related all that had happened since he left. He told them what he had learned of the Minoans. Then Pharon and Nessia filled in with many other stories of the life and history of their people.

Suddenly, as they talked, Cathy glanced at Crane. He had fallen sound asleep.

9

CRANE SLEPT for ten hours. When he went up to the control room the *Seaview* was well out to sea, and they were running on the surface for maximum speed. The detector was still locked on the *Theseus*. If all went well they should overtake Marpen in less than forty hours at a distance of four to five hundred miles from the Florida coast.

During the night Pharon's scientists had been showing the *Seaview* technicians the neutralizing apparatus and explaining its installation. The problems were not quite as simple as Pharon had apparently believed. Small units had to be installed at intervals throughout the ship. These required the running of a network of cables. Spare conduits existed in some areas of the ship, but in others there was none, and the cables had to pass through watertight bulkheads. The crews of technicians spread throughout the ship and began an around-the-clock modification program.

After a complete study of the system, Chief Engineer Halpert reported to Crane and Nelson. "It looks as if the apparatus will work, all right," he said. "There's only one thing wrong. It's going to take about twice as long as we've got to get it ready. We can overtake the *Theseus*, but the neutralizer won't be ready."

"It has to be!" said Nelson. "What do you need?"

"More men. More time."

"More time we can't give you. But we can give you every able-bodied man aboard, including the helmsmen. The ship can run on autopilot most of the way."

"That will help. But we'll still have to cut corners."

"Cut them. Tell Pharon's men the problem. They must be able to find ways to cut the time.

Crane and I and every other man aboard are at your disposal. Just show us what you need done."

Halpert's acceptance of their offer was instantaneous. He put them to work drilling holes in the hard steel of the bulkheads and installing watertight conduits. By lunchtime that day they had graduated to installation of neutralizer units under the guidance of Pharon's scientists. This was a critical operation, requiring extreme precision to establish the giant magnetic fields in the right phase relationship to absorb the destroying energy that Marpen would hurl at them.

In addition each torpedo had to be fitted with a small neutralizer unit, but every inch of space was already crammed with propulsion and guidance machinery. Yet room had to be found for a cubic foot of neutralizer.

At Halpert's recommendation, Crane put half his sweating crew of technicians on the modification of the torpedoes. The delicate inertial guidance systems of these deadly weapons had to be removed and replaced, and the power supplies had to be relocated to make room for the neutralizer. The engineers who designed and built the torpedoes would have been horrified at the precision assembly and alignment tasks the submarine crewmen were setting for themselves for an impossibly short time.

Halpert knew how to do it. He had a crew of a dozen expert machinists to build the necessary jigs and fixtures for realigning the guidance systems of the torpedoes. He drove them without mercy. From the rest of the crew he demanded equal performance. For the present, he was literally in command of the ship. If the necessary tasks required by Crane and Nelson did not get done, it would not be Halpert's fault.

They worked fifteen hours straight. The least technically qualified members of the crew served meals to the others at their work stations, assisted by Cathy and Nessia.

Then Crane gave orders for them to knock it off for a few hours of sleep. Further driving in their fatigued condition would only result in careless work, some of which had already appeared,

requiring laborious rework.

In the nervous tension they were under, some of them roused after only three or four hours of sleep. All of the rest were wakened by an alarm after five hours.

The units of the submarine system were completely installed after another ten hours, but the work on the torpedoes was far behind. Six of the twelve weapons carried by the *Seaview* were in various stages of dismantling, but the neutralizer units were not in place in any of them.

"We're not going to make it," said Halpert at last. "You can see what we're up against, Admiral. These things just aren't going together fast enough."

Nelson could see that what the chief engineer said was true. He glanced at the clock on the bulkhead. Ten hours until they closed with the *Theseus*. An additional four hours could perhaps be gained by slowing and allowing Marpen to approach nearer the coast. But that was the absolute maximum, and it was risky.

And it was not going to be enough—not at

the rate they were going.

The technicians and machinists were doing their best, but there were only a limited number who could do the delicate work required. And these were dead on their feet.

"Knock it off," said Nelson wearily to the sweating crew. "Run in your second team, Halpert. We'll keep the work going."

"Honest, Admiral, we can make it," one of the young technicians, Albertson, said earnestly. "Let us keep going."

Nelson smiled. "Thanks, sailor, but I want you for a second round. Take a break for an hour. We'll keep trying."

The admiral went forward and stared out the bow ports at the rushing, heaving sea. Crane was there, and Pharon. Nessia stood near with Sea Baby. Banks seemed to be constantly at her elbow assisting with the baby or in other ways. Crane wondered a bit about the bachelor geologist.

"It looks as if we've lost the ball game," said Crane. "But there must be some way out. We could notify the authorities to evacuate Miami and surrounding areas."

"We haven't time to convince them they should," said Nelson. "And if we did, more people would be killed in the resulting panic than will be in Marpen's earthquake."

"I doubt that," said Crane, "but you're probably right about the matter of convincing them. There must be other ways of attacking the *Theseus*."

"Depth charges," said Nelson. "But Marpen could knock out any boat we brought up before it had a chance to drop the ash cans."

Pharon nodded. "He could do that. But what about planes? Could you get planes to drop the charges?"

"The Sub Patrol!" Crane exclaimed.

Nelson looked at him. "Do you want the job of persuading them to come out and attack?"

"Why shouldn't they? What—" Crane paused. "I think I see what you mean," he said finally.

"I've been thinking of the Patrol ever since I came up here," said Nelson. "I've been trying to

think both of ways to avoid calling on them—
and of ways to persuade them to help. I've thought
of neither. But I believe they're our only
chance—and a very slim one."

The admiral stepped to the control desk and
called the radio room. "I would like to reach
Admiral T. J. Radcliffe of the Submarine Patrol
at Naval Headquarters," he said. "Use Naval
code scramble on voice channel. I'll take it here
in the observation room. If the admiral is not
there, have him located for emergency contact."

Nelson forced himself to sit in one of the chairs
before the ports. He closed his eyes and leaned
his head back to try to relax and allow his mental
machinery to function. There must be a solution
to the problem which he had not considered. He
did not know what it was.

He jerked back to attention as the radio
operator called out over the intercom. "Admiral
Nelson. Admiral Radcliffe on the circuit, sir."

Nelson strode to the desk and picked up the
phone. "Tom—this is Harriman. How are you?"

"Great. Where are you? When are we going

to get together for that marlin fishing we promised ourselves three years ago?"

"When we retire, I guess, the way things have been shaping up for us."

"What can I do for you, Harriman? They told me you were on a Class A emergency call. What's up?"

"You're aware, I'm sure," said Nelson, "of details of the disasters at Oil City Eighteen, the Corbazzi Mines, the North Sea gas field—"

"Yes, and the Anatolia Copper Mines," said Radcliffe. "An attempt was made to reach you, but the Institute said you were maintaining complete silence. You should have kept a listening watch."

"We had our hands full, Tom. We've found the cause of those disasters. They are not natural. They are man-made."

"What! Can you prove it?"

"We have all the proof we need. The source is aboard an enemy submarine. This ship is now headed for the east coast of Florida for the purpose of attacking surface cities in the very same manner. They intend to strike Miami first."

"What submarine? What nationality? How do they cause such a disastrous effect?"

"I'm not going to attempt to answer any of those questions, Tom. There isn't time. The submarine has got to be stopped before it gets within attack distance of the coast."

"Do you intend to attack it? You are fully armed, aren't you?"

"We're armed. But they have a weapon that makes our conventional torpedoes useless. We're trying to modify them, but we haven't time to complete. I want you to call out the Submarine Patrol and depth charge at the position we will give you."

There was silence. Both Crane and Nelson knew what it meant.

"Harriman," said Admiral Radcliffe, "can you imagine me going up to the White House to request authority to destroy a submarine belonging to an unnamed foreign nation on the basis that it is reportedly responsible for some disasters in a way presently unknown to science—and when that submarine has committed no proved overt act against the United States?"

Nelson took a deep breath of resignation. This was the answer he had known would be coming.

"There isn't time to go to the White House —or anywhere else," he said.

"You mean you'd ask me—on my own authority—to bomb a foreign submarine on your word that it intends to attack?"

"Yes," said Nelson.

"You know I can't do it. I have authority to destroy any submarine that is guilty of hostile activity. But a preventive bombing—you are asking me to risk a war with a foreign power and destroy my career. Yet you offer no details!"

"The owner of this submarine is a band of renegades rather than a responsible governmental authority. They possess only one ship. When it is destroyed, they are through. But they have the power to do what I have told you."

"Harriman, you're asking me to believe the impossible."

"Yes," said Nelson slowly, "I guess I am—"

"I've known you as a responsible naval officer

twenty-five years. We've been personal friends for that long. You built the *Seaview* as the greatest submarine of all time and the first nonmilitary vessel of its kind. You've performed invaluable service with it whenever called upon."

"I guess I've earned my share of little gold stars," said Nelson.

"Shut up! What I'm trying to say is that I've either got to believe that what you say is true or that you've gone off your rocker. You've put me in a devil of a spot, Harriman!"

"I intended to."

"All right. The closest Sub Patrol will be ordered out on an armed alert exercise. They will be directed to drop live ammunition at the designated spot. You and I will either rid the seas of a menace—or we will be responsible for starting a war! And when this is over you'd better have a first-rate story to tell me!"

Nelson exhaled with unbelieving relief. "You won't regret it, Tom."

"The position, bearing, and velocity of the target, man!"

Quickly Nelson read off the required information.

He gave orders to the radio operator to keep the channel constantly available for communication with Admiral Radcliffe.

"Now," Nelson said, "we'll continue work on the torpedoes as if our conversation with the admiral had never taken place. We'll do everything humanly possible to take care of the situation if he fails."

Halpert regrouped his forces, concentrating his best men on two of the torpedoes to assure their completion first. It began to look better to him. He predicted completion of those two if the *Seaview* delayed contact with the *Theseus* for the additional four hours they now contemplated.

Nelson estimated it would require less than an hour for the Sub Patrol to respond to the alert. He ordered a radar watch posted to pick up the Patrol planes when they showed up. Almost immediately, the operator reported their presence.

"Patrol on screen, sir. Three planes. Ten minutes from target."

Nelson would have liked a direct contact from
the *Seaview* to the Patrol planes, but he didn't
dare risk giving the pilots that much indication
that this was any more than a purely routine
alert. The order to drop live ash cans was enough
to excite their suspicions.

The radio operator tuned in the code-scram-
bled channels on which the planes and the headquarters were communicating. The channels from
the *Seaview* to the headquarters were also open
now, and continuous corrections to the course
and range of the *Theseus* were being given to
headquarters for relay to the Patrol planes.

"Almost there," the radar operator said. The
blips of the planes nearly coincided with the position of the *Theseus* supplied to the radar screen
by the magnetic detection instruments.

The voice of the bombardier on the lead Patrol plane droned off his position. "Start bomb
run. Ten seconds now."

Crane could imagine the crew. Young, tense,

alert. They had never seen war, but they would be wondering if they were seeing it now. Yet they would know in their hearts that it could be nothing more than a practice alert.

The bomb run had started for the lead plane. It was halfway through. In a moment the radar would pick up the blips of the falling depth charges as the plane wheeled away from them.

Suddenly from the planes there came a tremendous roar that was as abruptly cut off. The control room became strangely quiet. Then Kinning, the radar operator, cried out, "One of them's gone! There are only two Patrol planes!"

The radio channel came alive again. The pilot of the second plane was calling headquarters. "Robin One Wye to Headquarters. Robin One Zee disintegrated in midair explosion near end of bomb run. No apparent cause. Robin One Wye starting bomb run. Ten seconds."

The second Patrol plane did not even reach the halfway point of its run when the sound blast struck again.

"The second plane," the radar operator cried.

"The second plane has disappeared!"

From the headquarters channel came the urgent thunder of Admiral Radcliffe's voice. "Turn back! Robin One Ex, turn back!"

It was too late. The lone blip on the radar screen made a slow turn to retrace its course. Then it, too, vanished.

"All of them," Nelson exclaimed in despair. "Marpen got all three planes! How did he do it?"

Pharon was staring at the screen. "I don't understand," he murmured. "Marpen's weapon creates a field that would extend only weakly above the surface. I know it would not be strong enough to destroy those planes."

"The planes were destroyed by an explosion," said Crane. "I think I know what caused it. The depth charges have pressure triggers which fire when the cans sink to a depth where the pressure actuates them. The magneto-gravity field created by the *Theseus* was strong enough to trigger the depth charges."

"You're right," said Nelson. "We should have

been able to anticipate that."

Almost unheard, the voice of Admiral Radcliffe thundered over the loudspeaker. "Harriman! Did you see that? What happened to my
planes? What did your target do to them?"

Nelson picked up the microphone wearily.
"They have a pressure field. We underestimated
its effect, but it was sufficient to trigger the depth
charges carried by the planes. We are to blame
for not recognizing the danger."

"This is no time to be concerned about blame.
That ship has now committed an overt act. We'll
have destroyers intercept its path. We'll fly Patrol planes so high they can't possibly touch
them."

"No," said Nelson.

"What do you mean, no? You got us started
on this thing. We're going to see it through."

"You can't risk any more planes and crews.
There's no more reason to think others could
get through, no matter how high they flew. If
they carry depth charges, they carry their own
destruction. Yet that's the only weapon they can

use against this ship. Subrocs would be destroyed long before they could do any damage."

"Then what are you going to do?" Radcliffe demanded. "What *can* you do?"

"We've got to get to him with a specially modified torpedo. There's not another thing in the world that will touch him."

10 Battle

W E'VE GOT *one* torpedo ready," said Halpert. "We've run into snags on the other. It'll be one to two hours before the second is checked out. Do you want to go with just one?"

Nelson, Crane, and Pharon looked at the haggard engineer and at each other. A single torpedo against the *Theseus*. Each knew it was total folly to engage the *Theseus* with no more ammunition than this. But each knew what their answer had to be.

"I think this has to be your decision, Admiral," said Crane.

"You're the skipper," said Nelson. "But if you ask for my vote, I say we go."

Crane nodded. "There isn't any other answer.

Get your fish ready to shoot, Halpert. And keep the crew going on the other one. Maybe by the time we close up, it will be ready."

Halpert shook his head. "It won't be."

The torpedoes had every kind of guidance in the modern arsenal of weaponry. They would seek a source of heat, sound, light, magnetism, or a huge mass such as the *Theseus*. But the seamen had no way of predicting the effect of the tremendous field of the *Theseus* on these guidance mechanisms.

The *Seaview* had been closing rapidly for some time. Marpen was almost at the minimum distance from the Florida coast which they dared permit before attacking. Crane gave the command, "Battle stations!" over the intercom. It was not an unfamiliar cry, for all of *Seaview's* crewmen were former Navy men, and they were accustomed to frequent drills aboard the *Seaview*.

The crewmen assumed their posts quietly and reported in sequence to Crane. "Reactor room is ready, sir!" "Diving station one manned and ready, sir!"

And the final, important one: "Torpedo room manned and ready, sir! Number three tube ready to fire!"

Number three tube, Crane thought grimly. Number three was all. The other eleven were useless or empty. If number three missed, what second chance would they have?

Marpen must know by now that he was followed. Pharon believed Marpen would have guessed it was the *Seaview* and that Marpen was waiting for them to approach close enough for a quick kill.

Pharon's technicians were assigned to the control board to watch the neutralizer indicators. They did not speak English, of course, but Pharon relayed their comments.

"They've definitely picked us up now," said the Minoan chief technician. "The field is intensifying on our bearing. It's approaching attack level."

"What is our range?" Crane asked.

"Eighteen miles," the detector operator reported quickly.

"We'll close to five before we release the torpedo. These long-range torpedoes are good for
a lot more than that, but we've got only one
chance."

"Attack level!" announced the chief technician.

The seamen looked apprehensively at the walls
and ceiling of the room about them. They re-
called vividly the tortured wrenching and twisting that shook the *Seaview* in the harbor of Minos. But now there was no noticeable vibration or
disturbance of any kind. It was hard to believe
that twisting, tearing force was surging through
the sea around them.

"The neutralizers are holding," said Pharon.
"What is their present ratio of absorption?"

"Six percent," said the technician.

Pharon made a quick mental calculation. "At
this present rate, the neutralizers will be safely
within capacity at five miles. They will begin to
overload near four miles. There is very little
margin of safety there. And this is based on the
supposition that Marpen does not increase the

field intensity. If he does, you'll have to release the torpedo at a greater distance."

"We'll ride it this way unless something changes," said Crane. "Let me know at once if there is any increase in field intensity."

Pharon relayed the request to his technicians. In silence the group watched the instruments as the *Seaview* sped closer to the enemy vessel. The field intensified because of the change in distance, but the neutralizers continued to soak up the killing energy.

Crane moved to the torpedo firing station and fingered the controls. It seemed too easy, after all, he thought. It was hard to believe success was this close.

"Range!" called the navigation officer.

Crane tripped the torpedo release. The reaction of the ejection sent a faint jar throughout the ship. The helmsman swung the rudder full right. On the indicator screens a new blip of light appeared, marking the trail of the destruction that bore toward the *Theseus*.

Marpen's crew must have seen it, too, for the

Theseus suddenly zigged to a new course. As if tied to it by a leash, the torpedo obediently followed.

"Right on course!" the Minoan chief technician exclaimed.

One mile.

Two. Crane let out a long-held breath.

Not quite three—

The blip of light never reached the three-mile mark. It suddenly flared to a wider spread and died. Then the *Seaview* was battered by a thunderous explosion that rammed through the sea and smashed against the steel hull. The submarine heeled over, spilling its crew against the hull and bulkheads and throwing them into the control panels. Here and there lights died.

Slowly the great ship righted itself. The officers and men at all stations scrambled to their feet and sought their operating posts. An emergency battery-powered light flashed on automatically. Crane reached the intercom. "All stations report!"

Water was coming in an aft storage compartment. It had already been sealed off by a watertight bulkhead door. Engines and controls had withstood the shock except for minor external damage to knobs and levers when the crewmen were thrown against them.

The bow planesman hesitated, checked his controls once more, and reported, "Bow plane damaged by shock wave. Port side."

The *Seaview* had continued its tight turn. Now it headed away from the *Theseus* at top speed. When they were past the fifteen-mile mark Crane turned to his companions in resignation.

"That was our wad. We shot it and muffed. What went wrong?"

"Some defect in the torpedo," said Nelson. "Maybe we created it by our modification. But we can't stop. We've got to get that second fish ready. We've got to keep on until Marpen is right up on the beach."

"He doesn't have to be," said Crane. "Twenty miles away is close enough for him, according to the Minoans."

"That is correct," said Pharon. "But I think you are wrong about the torpedo. It was detonated by an outside force, and the only outside force present was the field from the *Theseus*. I think your recording charts will show that at the moment of explosion a tremendous increase of field intensity was applied directly to the torpedo. The neutralizer unit in the weapon was not sufficient in capacity to absorb it."

"Then we never had a chance—and we haven't got one now!" said Crane. "All we can do is sit here and watch Marpen tear an American city to shreds!"

"I underestimated the power Marpen could bring to bear on the torpedo," said Pharon. "Our neutralizers for the torpedoes were not built large enough to handle it."

"It's not your fault," said Nelson. "We'll always be grateful for the effort you have made.

"But we can't let Marpen escape. It isn't just one city—it may be a hundred. It's not just one nation—it's the whole world. He'll keep on destroying until destruction overtakes him. There's one thing yet that we can do: load the bow of the *Seaview* with nuclear warheads and ram through a collision with him. No matter if we don't reach him. Such a blast will destroy him —as well as us."

"The price might not be too high," said Pharon slowly. "But I think there may be one slightly less desperate way, although the risk is almost as great as trying to ram the *Theseus*."

"What is it?" Nelson demanded. "Time is gone. The only measures we can try now are desperate ones."

"Your second torpedo must be almost ready," said Pharon. "Instead of mounting one of the small neutralizer units in it, let us install one of the units from the submarine itself. Unless Marpen can use a field of unbelievable capacity, that unit should protect the torpedo."

"And what about the submarine?" asked Crane.

"That is the risk," said Pharon. "With a portion of the neutralizer protection gone, the ship could be vulnerable to the field of the *Theseus*."

"Would we have a chance to get within range to fire the torpedo before we got shaken to pieces?"

"I am certain we could approach to the necessary range. How much damage we might suffer I cannot tell."

"Let's try it," said Nelson, "with one modification. Let's bring six nuclear warheads from the torpedoes into the observation room. Wire them for manual detonation, but arrange that they can also be fired by shock detonation—if and after we learn that the torpedo has failed. Agreed?"

They looked from the admiral to each other. They nodded slowly.

"Your crewmen—" Pharon said. "They should be told. They should have a chance."

"I'll tell them," Nelson said grimly. "But there's no chance of separating out those who want to back out. We're running under pressurization. Even if rescue means were at hand, there's no way to get them out and depressurized safely. We're all in this together, and it looks as if we have just one more go at it."

While changes were being made in the second torpedo, and the neutralizer unit was being stripped from the submarine, Nelson called all off-duty crewmen to the main wardroom. He switched the intercom to all other compartments of the ship. Then he told them briefly and carefully the situation they were in and the decision that had been made.

"There is an out for at least ten men," Nelson said. "No more. The minisub will hold that many in an emergency. Those who wish to leave can drop their names in this box, which I'm going to leave in my room. If there are more than ten, lots will be drawn to see who gets the minisub. That's all, men."

A half hour later he looked in the box. There were no names there. He had known there wouldn't be.

He tried to argue with himself that they should do something less desperate. They should retreat and learn the secret of the neutralizers and attack the *Theseus* at another time and another place, with enough armament to make certain she would never forage the seas again.

But—before that time Miami would be crushed, a million people would die. And how many other cities would fall before they could arm and find the *Theseus* again?

It had to be now.

There was one more thing they could do, however. Nelson called Admiral Radcliffe again. His fellow admiral was scarcely in a mood to talk, but Nelson got him to respond to a request to put a tape recorder on the channel.

"It's already on," said Radcliffe. "I want all the evidence I can get when it comes to sorting out things when this is all over."

"Good," said Nelson. "I'm not going to tell you what my next move is, but I'm going to put on someone who can give you the full technical details of these weapons I've been talking about. We've got only a couple of hours. It will be all over then."

He put on Pharon and the Minoan scientists. They gave the theory behind the generation of magneto-gravity fields, the means of building generators, and the design of neutralizers to defend against the fields.

When they were through Nelson was certain that naval scientists could build a defense that would eventually destroy Marpen and his *Theseus* even if the *Seaview* failed.

Halpert's crew had finished. Their torpedo had been tested and was as perfect as they knew how to make it. They hoisted it into number three tube.

The *Seaview* had been turned around once again and was closing slowly on the *Theseus*. The Minoan submarine was close to the continental shelf, and it was here, rather than at the coast itself, that the attack would be made, according to Pharon.

While the torpedo had been in process of modification, six nuclear warheads had been brought into the observation room and lashed to the floor at the bow. Electric circuits were installed to explode them at the press of a trigger—two triggers in reality. Crane and Nelson were each to hold one. A decision to fire would be their joint decision. If the torpedo was blown up prematurely by Marpen the shock would detonate the warheads.

While final checks were under way, the sonar operator called out. "Something on the sonar— I can't make out what it is."

"Earth vibrations!" cried Pharon. "Marpen has begun his attack on the city!"

The *Theseus* had slowed to a near stop, but the *Seaview* still had ten miles to close range. Crane ordered the turbine room, "Full speed."

In the control room all eyes were on the sonar record. The crewmen listened to the throbbing, pulsing thunder generated in the seabed by the *Theseus*. They did not know how long it took such pounding energy to build up earth tremors capable of toppling the great buildings of Miami. Maybe it was already happening.

"Contact! We're in their field," the technician suddenly announced.

Simultaneously the sonar recording diminished. "He's withdrawing his energy there and putting it into a beam on us," said Pharon.

"At least we have drawn their fire," said Crane. "Now to see if we can take it."

They remained quiet. They could already feel a throb in the ship. It was a steady pounding that shook the deck plates under their feet, now this way, now that.

As the *Seaview* closed swiftly, terrible vibrations built up in her hull and wracked the structure of her machinery. In the observation room all eyes drifted to the six ominous shapes of the warheads lashed to the floor.

The full fury of the *Theseus* was turned against the *Seaview* now. The meters showed that Marpen had increased the energy of his attack considerably over that of their previous encounter. This meant that the neutralizer system would have been overloaded at five miles if in perfect condition. Now, with one unit subtracted, and the rest thrown out of balance by its absence—

"Overload!" The Minoan chief technician called out.

Crane and Nelson accepted the information

wordlessly. The *Seaview* bore on, its structure wracked by the twisting, tearing forces of magnetism and gravity that Marpen hurled at them.

Crane glanced at the range reading. "Ready for firing," he called. "Helmsman, do not—repeat —do not turn after firing. Continue steady on course at quarter speed."

Crane kept his eyes on the instruments. The shaking of the deck almost threw him into the panel. The range crept down. Four and eight-tenths. Four and six. Four and five—

Crane squeezed the release.

The torpedo's ejection was scarcely felt in the shuddering, wrenching ship. But the crewmen saw its blip on the instrument screens. It crawled slowly across the narrow space separating the two submarines.

Crane caught Nelson's eye and threw the switch that turned on the impact detonation circuits of the nuclear warheads beside them. If the *Theseus* exploded the torpedo at an ineffective distance the blast would set off the nuclear warheads in the *Seaview*.

Only if the torpedo reached the *Theseus* would its blast level be low enough not to set off the warheads.

The *Theseus* shifted abruptly in its course. The blip of the torpedo followed—followed and closed.

The spot of light blossomed on the screen. Crane's hand swept down to deactivate the warhead circuits that would never be needed now.

"Down!" he cried. "All down!"

He threw himself to the deck, but it seemed as if the deck rose halfway to meet him. There was a deep and awful roaring that filled the universe before darkness and silence closed over him.

11

THE *SEAVIEW* raced eastward on the surface through the heavy, wallowing seas of a South Atlantic storm. Repairs of the extensive damage done to the submarine had taken three days, two of which had been spent with the reactor shut down. Fortunately the repairs could be completed at sea.

From radio reports the crew learned that damage to Miami had been relatively slight. A couple of hotels had been cracked so badly they would have to be taken down. Others could be repaired. Only a handful of lives had been lost, and a few score injured.

The great explosion at the edge of the continental shelf off Miami remained a mystery.

Ships and submarines had gone to investigate. Evidence of radioactivity had been found. But there was no explanation.

Outside the *Seaview* only Admiral Radcliffe knew the story. "I hope what you are telling me is one hundred percent truth," he said grimly to Crane and Nelson as the *Seaview* headed for Minos. "If this should turn out to be a ship of a major power, we've got a war on our hands."

"You'll never hear of the incident again," Nelson promised. "I regret the loss of the Patrol planes, but, considering the whole cost, I assure you we came out very cheaply in the whole affair."

"I can only take your word for it at the moment," said Radcliffe. "I haven't made any disposition of those tapes yet. Some serious thought needs to be given that matter. When are you coming in?"

"We'll try to contact you within two weeks. We're taking Pharon and his people home now."

The *Seaview* cut off. Nelson looked at Crane, and they were thinking the same thing. They wished now that Radcliffe didn't have those tapes. What was revealed there was too terrible a weapon for any nation's knowledge. Somehow they would have to try to get them, but they didn't think they would have much luck.

They reached the African continental shelf and submerged to the level of the caverns of Minos. Slowly they penetrated the undersea passage again and surfaced in the quiet harbor.

Crane turned on the periscope. The view of the city and the quay flashed on the screens.

For a moment they studied it with dismay. Then Crane uttered the thought that struck them all. "Something looks wrong. There aren't any people—only those few on the dock. The place looks—deserted!"

"Yes. Something's very much wrong," said Pharon in great agitation. "It's never like that. The streets should be filled with people. I must get ashore at once."

The hatches were quickly opened. A boat had put out from the dock and pulled alongside the submarine. Pharon descended and engaged in sharp conversation with the two Minoan boat-men. Then he returned to the deck of the *Seaview*.

"You've got to get all your men out immediately!" he exclaimed to Crane and Nelson. "At once—there's no time to lose. Boats will be provided—"

"Wait a minute!" said Crane. "What are you talking about? We're not leaving the *Seaview*."

"The cavern—it's going to be blasted and sealed. The charges are already set with time releases. My people overthrew Marpen's followers after our departure and determined to seal Minos forever from the outside world. If it had been the *Theseus* returning it would have been buried in the collapsing cavern. Since it was the *Seaview* they have given time enough for us to get out and join the others in the cities beyond. But this city has been abandoned and will be buried forever, along with the undersea channel. You can do nothing about the *Seaview*, but you can get all your men away. But hurry!"

Even after the terrors they had seen in past

days, it was hard to comprehend what Pharon was telling them. Nelson loked up at the distant rock ceiling above them, with its marvelous artificial sky. He looked out along the long hull of the *Seaview*, the ultimate achievement of his lifetime.

"Can we ever return to the surface?" Crane was saying. "Is there any way back for us?"

"There is no present route. But in the future —surely we can prepare a way. We can do that in return for all you have done."

The future, thought Crane. Years, perhaps. Most of the remaining life of some of them—

"How long have we got?" Nelson demanded.

"Minutes!" said Pharon desperately. "No more than time to pass those farthest hills into the valley cavern beyond. You've got to get your men out here at once."

Other boats were coming now, bumping against the hull of the *Seaview*, ready to take the men off.

"That's at least an hour's hike," said Nelson. "We took two hours and eighteen minutes coming through the passage on manual and sonar control. But we've got tapes of our two trips in and one out. We can tie the tapes into the computer and use the sonar to monitor and we can go out on autopilot at least twice as fast as we came in.

"We'll put it up to the men. Those who want to stay can do so. If there's enough of a crew left to run the ship we'll try to get the *Seaview* out."

Nelson disappeared into the hull.

Pharon shook his head in despair. "You haven't time. It's suicide to attempt to run the channel. The outer orifice will be shattered before you can possibly reach it."

"We think it's worth a try," said Crane. "You have no idea how fast this boat can get through that channel when she puts her little old tin brain to it."

Nessia was on deck with the prince. Cathy, beside her, clasped them both in farewell. Banks stood behind them.

Nelson appeared through the conning-tower door once more. "If any are staying they should be up here by now. I take it we're sailing with a full crew. Wish us luck, Pharon—Nessia. There are a million things we should have talked about. And now we never can—"

Pharon caught the hands of each of them. "Good luck to you, then. May your gods and mine watch over you."

Cathy hugged Nessia once more and darted inside. The eyes of both women were wet. Nelson gave a final look around. Banks was still out.

"I'm going to stay, Admiral—Captain," he said abruptly. "Thanks for everything—"

Nelson stared incredulously. "You're what?"

"I have nothing back there. No people. No possessions. It's the dream of a lifetime here, this world of the Minoans. I have a chance to learn more than all the scholars of the world can ever know about this great people."

Then Crane and Nelson saw that Nessia was standing by, waiting for Banks to come.

The geologist saw their glance. He smiled confidently. "Yes, I think I have someone here. Good luck to you all."

He waved and leaped with Nessia to the boat, never looking back as it slid across the harbor. Crane watched for an instant in utter bafflement. But it began to make sense. He remembered how it had been aboard the submarine. Half the time Banks had been holding the baby or doing some other small courtesy for Nessia. He hoped it worked out well for them.

"Are we going, sailor?" Nelson was halfway into the submarine.

"Yes, sir! You bet we are!" shouted Crane.

They were three-fourths of the way through the undersea channel when the first violent blast struck. It was ahead of them, near the entrance. The second blast was in the rear and rolled them as if a depth charge had burst on top of them. Thousands of tons of rock were torn loose from the roof and sides of the cavern and slid into the water. The *Seaview* reeled and shook from the impact. Her forward motion all but ceased.

The terrible assault ended, but the deck tilted crazily and did not right itself. Crane did not know if they were still afloat or had been forced to the bottom and buried there.

"All compartments report. Diving station report!"

"Buoyancy lost. We're descending. One-hundred ten feet above seabed. Diving planes damaged all around."

"Pump ballast. Regain previous level."

Leakage was reported aft and was sealed off.

Crane inquired, "Any channel ahead?"

"None at all," the sonar operator reported. "Completely blocked."

At that moment the third blast came. It was very far behind them, but the *Seaview* rocked with the impact of it. And suddenly the ship lightened and began rising rapidly. The tanks were quickly opened to admit more ballast.

"Something was on our back—rocks and debris," said Nelson. "That last blast must have shaken it off."

And now, as far as they knew, the channel was blocked both in front and behind them. They were trapped eleven hundred feet beneath the surface of the sea.

Crane ordered the diving officer, "Adjust buoyancy and hold to twenty feet off the cavern roof." This would be a near-impossible maneuver, and no one knew it more than Crane.

He ordered the helmsman, "Patrol the face of the cave-in ahead of us at minimum speed."

To the sonar operator he said, "We want a profile of the cave-in. Try for every possible point where a breakthrough may still exist."

Slowly, ponderously, the giant submarine edged along the face of the cave-in, as if snuffing her way here and there, searching for the hoped-for passage that might still remain. During the next half hour repeated blasts reverberated through the rocks and the water, becoming ever more distant and then ceasing altogether.

It was too late now to do anything, Nelson thought. They had almost made it out. But now the whole cavern and all the wondrous city they had seen was buried forever. Like themselves?

The search was finished, and the seamen bent over the records.

"One hole," said the sonar operator. "Not

more than ten feet high and fifteen wide."

"And we need eighty feet to get the *Seaview* through like a thread in a needle," said Crane. "Look. Suppose this stuff that's fallen has piled up like a load of sand dumped from a truck. That would mean it's roughly conical with a peak that's maybe not too thick. If so, we might be able to do something about it."

"What are you suggesting?" asked Nelson.

"Put a torpedo into it—with a conventional warhead—and see if we can flatten it enough to let us through."

Nelson straightened and looked at the group around him. "We haven't much to lose," he said.

The position of the narrow opening was marked, and the *Seaview* moved to the far limit of her confined area. It was hardly more than a half-mile. Crane ordered a final recheck, then gave the order.

The ejection of the torpedo was felt faintly. Moments later the blast came, thundering again against their already battered hull.

A complete compartment check showed no damage. Crane checked with the sonar operator. "How does it look?"

The man hesitated. "Like the eye of a needle, sir!"

They had three feet of vertical clearance at the tightest point. It was absolute insanity to try to take a ship like the *Seaview* through such a channel, even if the planes had been working.

The ship literally slid through on her belly. They dared not lighten the ballast enough to give even the slightest chance of scraping the roof and bringing down more tons of rock.

And the piled-up rock in the channel hadn't fallen like a cone. It stretched for hundreds of yards, but miraculously the opening enlarged as they passed through. The searchlights in the bow showed jagged rocks over which they must pass, any one of which could pierce the pressure hull like a needle in a balloon if a sudden current or mistake in ballasting brought the *Seaview* down hard.

It was a three-hour nightmare.

And then they were in the sea once more.

They decompressed the interior of the ship as rapidly as they dared. When they surfaced and came out through open hatches once more in the middle of the Atlantic, it was night. The stars and the moon were bright. Only faint wisps of clouds crossed them, and the sea was as smooth as it ever was.

The *Seaview* rode the waves with light, graceful plunges as she homed at top speed, the realm of the Sea Kings behind her forever.

"It never happened," said Cathy as she stood with Lee Crane on the bridge in the conning tower. "In a little while we'll wake up and know it was all a dream."

Crane held out his lean, hard hand. "Dreams don't leave you with the permanent shakes like this. Or they don't whiten the fuzz like this!" He removed his cap and brushed his coal-black hair.

Cathy laughed and gently put her arms around his neck. "You'll recover, Captain. I'm sure you'll recover and sail your ship another day."